AND OTHER STORIES

DARK SPACES

AND OTHER STORIES

BY ALAN GIBBONS AND ROBBIE GIBBONS

WITH ILLUSTRATIONS BY ROBBIE GIBBONS

CABOODLE BOOKS LTD

A Catalogue record for this book is available from the
British Library.

ISBN-13: 978-0-9559711-4-3

Typeset in ITC Garamond by www.envydesign.co.uk

Printed in the UK by CPI Cox & Wyman, Reading

Caboodle Books Ltd
Riversdale, 8 Rivock Avenue, Steeton, BD20 6SA
Tel: 01535 656015

CONTENTS

THE BLOOD MARKET

BY ALAN GIBBONS

There he was again, the man in the fedora hat. It reminded me of a cowboy hat but it was black. I averted my gaze for at least ninety seconds before stealing a wary look in his direction. Immediately, my heart leapt. He was still watching, staring right at me. The moment his colourless eyes held mine, I turned my back on him, willing that inhuman stare to loosen its icy grip.

"Something wrong?"

The questioner was a plump, middle-aged woman standing just a couple of metres away. She seemed to have materialised from nowhere. She was wearing jeans, a faded jacket and a bobble hat, a bit of an eccentric if you ask me.

"Not really," I confessed nervously, still uncomfortably aware of the watching stranger.

The woman frowned and allowed her stare to stray over my shoulder. There was a flicker of recognition in her eyes.

"It's Billy Scarecrow there, isn't it?" she asked. "He's the one who's got you spooked."

"Yes," I said, "he's been following me round for the last ten minutes."

"Has he indeed?" she asked, raising an eyebrow.

"Is that his name?" I enquired. "Billy Scarecrow?"

At that, she roared with laughter, her stocky frame quivering.

"Now wouldn't that be something?" she chortled. "Scarecrow by name, scarecrow by nature. No, that's just the name we give him."

I found myself wondering who she meant by *we*. She was on her own.

"Believe me," she added, "he's no friend of mine."

I felt stupid for thinking Billy Scarecrow was his real name.

"I've seen him around though," she said. "Him and his kind use the Flea Market and other public places for their dirty business."

That made Billy Scarecrow sound like some kind of crook. I wondered what his particular line of crime could be. Whatever it was, the Flea Market would be a good cover. It's been held every Sunday for as long as anyone can remember. It draws big crowds down to Coogan's Row, local people and tourists alike. I continued to wonder what the woman meant by 'dirty business' but she made no effort to explain herself.

"Is he still there?" I asked.

Once more, she peered over my shoulder.

"Yes, he's there, large as life and twice as ugly."

I shuddered. Ugly was right. The watcher was tall and lean, a wolf of a man. He had to be at least six feet six. He was built like a skeleton but there was power in that gaunt frame. Rat tails of greasy blond hair spilled from the brim of his battered Fedora hat. His shapeless coat hung from broad shoulders, reaching down below his knees. But none of that had affected me in the least. It was his eyes and his complexion that had affected me so dramatically. His eyes were fixed and without pigmentation, his skin pale and translucent. But he wasn't an albino. No, this was something altogether different.

"Are you on your own, son?" the woman asked.

I nodded.

"I came down here with a couple of mates," I told her. "Their parents have just picked them up."

"Leaving you on your own?"

"Yes," I told her. "I'm waiting for my Dad to show."

She frowned. "And old Billy Scarecrow's been giving you the heebie-jeebies?"

I forced out an uneasy laugh. "Got it in one."

"Don't you worry," she told me. "You stay here with me." She winked. "My name's Sally, by the way. Don't worry about a thing. You'll come to no harm with me beside you."

I found it hard to imagine what a little dumpling of a woman could do against Billy Scarecrow but he hadn't made a move yet.

"Is he still watching me?" I asked, not daring to look.

Sally ran her eyes over the crowd and shook her

head. The man in the fedora hat had gone. There was no sign of him. It was at that point Dad finally put in an appearance. He was making his way towards me through the crowd. I knew it would freak him out if he saw me talking to a stranger so I made my excuses to Sally.

"My Dad's here," I said. "Look, just forget all about it. I was probably imagining it anyway."

Sally shook her head. "I wish it was that easy."

There she goes again, I thought. First she hints at dirty business then this. There seemed to be an extra dimension to everything she said. Is she trying to tell me something, I wondered.

"Get yourself off home, son," Sally said. "And keep your eyes peeled. Remember, when he comes for you, he won't cast a shadow."

I stared at her for a moment. *When* he comes for me! What did she have to say that for? I was worried before. Now my skin was crawling with fright. I hurried away to meet Dad, forcing myself not to look back. It would only set her off again, coming out with her weird stuff.

"The car's over there," Dad said, oblivious to the strange characters that peopled the Flea Market. "Look lively. I'm parked on a yellow line."

I've never been so glad to get in the car. As I buckled up, I happened to glimpse movement in the wing mirror. It was him. The man in the fedora hat had just stepped out of the crowd. I twisted round to look at him, a shadowy figure in the dying light, standing as tall and still as a statue. As for Sally, she was nowhere to be seen. Meanwhile, Dad selected first gear and pulled out into the busy traffic. I continued to stare at Billy Scarecrow until he started to vanish into the twilight. But before he faded from sight completely, he left me a parting gift. As we reached the T-junction at the top of the road, he raised his right hand...and waved.

For the next few days I was haunted by the man in the fedora hat. Billy Scarecrow's colourless eyes floated through my nightmares. His skeletal frame cast a long shadow over my every thought. I would be sitting in class listening to one of my teachers and my stalker's face would explode into my mind like flash photography going off. I didn't tell anybody about him. Nobody would have taken me seriously anyway. The only person who believed me was Sally and she was utterly bonkers! The following Wednesday night I heard Mum commenting about an item on the BBC News bulletin.

"She's been missing for four days now," she said. "Just think about her poor parents. They look worried sick."

I looked up from my homework and stared at the screen. It was a police press conference. In the top right-hand corner of the screen there was a picture of a girl about my age in her school uniform. She was smiling slightly self-consciously.

"What is it?" I asked.

"That girl," Dad explained. "She's been missing ever since Sunday evening. She hasn't been home for three nights."

I read the girl's name on the strip at the bottom of the screen. She was called Katie Swallow. I watched her Mum and Dad making their halting, tearful appeal for their daughter's safe return.

"Since Sunday you say?"

"That's right," Mum answered. "She went to the Flea Market just like you did. Just think, you might have seen her around."

"But she never came home?" I asked.

Dad shook his head. "She went with a friend. The other girl popped into a shop to top up her mobile. By the time she came out, Katie had vanished."

I stared. There were too many similarities to what happened to me.

"She goes to St Teresa's," Dad added.

I swallowed hard. This really was all too close to home. St Teresa's High School for Girls is only half a mile from my school. I would see the girls every day getting on two bus stops after me in their blue uniforms.

"So don't complain about us picking you up from now on," Mum said. "There but for fortune."

I gave a bit of a half-nod. There but for fortune. Up in my room, I couldn't help but dwell on the news bulletin. A girl going missing the same day that creepazoid followed me round the Flea Market, it was no coincidence. It had to be after two in the morning before I managed to get off to sleep so it was hardly surprising that I was yawning all the way through breakfast.

"Were you up all hours playing on that computer again?" Mum demanded.

"No," I said, offended. "I couldn't get to sleep, that's all."

Mum gave me that sideways look of hers. She didn't believe me.

"Is there any news about that girl?" I asked. "Katie…"

I struggled to remember her second name.

"Katie Swallow," Mum said. "No, I'm afraid not. The police are searching those old warehouses down by Coogan's Row." She glanced at the kitchen clock. "Did you remember your Dad and I are going to be home later than usual this evening? His boss is having a retirement party. It shouldn't go on too long. We'll definitely be home by nine."

She told me where my tea would be, what temperature to set the dial and how long to leave it in the oven. She reminded me *three times* to turn it off when I'd finished. I was half way out of the door when she called me back.

"And don't forget," she said. "T.."

"I know," I snorted, rolling my eyes, "turn off the oven."

That evening all I could think about was that stupid oven. Mum always made me use the oven because she didn't trust me to microwave anything. I once left a metal spoon in something I was heating up. I nearly blew the house up and she's never going to let me forget it. I was just serving up the pasta when I glimpsed something outside. I looked across the street. There, in the halo of the street lamp, stood a silhouetted figure that made my heart stutter. It was him, the man in the fedora hat, Billy Scarecrow. What's more, he was staring straight at me. I looked at him so long the heat from the dish burned through the oven gloves. With a cry of pain, I let it fall on the floor. The dish smashed, spraying pasta and garlic sauce up the wall. I looked helplessly at the mess then glanced back at the window. He was gone.

Instantly, a disturbing thought buzzed through my

mind, the same thought I'd had when I heard Katie Swallow had gone missing from the Flea Market. This was no coincidence. I mean, what were the chances that, of all the houses in London, he would show up outside mine? In the same split second something even more worrying occurred to me. What if he was planning to break in?

I raced to the front door and put the bolts on, something we only usually did when we turned in for the night. That done, I raced to the back door and double-locked it, sliding the bolts across there too. My heart was pounding. What now?

I didn't have to wait long. While I was standing there in the kitchen I heard something, a relentless tap-tap-tap coming from the living room. My flesh crawled. I half-knew what to expect as I made my way towards the sound. Shoving open the door with my right hand, I stepped into the living room...and gasped. There he was, my stalker. Billy Scarecrow had his long, almost fleshless face pressed against the window pane. I noticed that his breath didn't cloud the glass. Simultaneously, I became aware of his fingers. They were long and tapering and tipped with curving, claw-like nails. Tap-tap-tap they went and his colourless eyes fixed me.

Let me in.

His lips weren't moving but that didn't stop his thoughts burrowing their way into my head.

Open the door and let me in.

The thin, pale lips peeled back to reveal a row of serrated, ivory-white fangs. They glinted evilly in the light cast by the living room light. My worst, unspoken fears had come true.

Open the door.

Let me in.

Each word crackled through my mind like a firework. I didn't move. I read somewhere that vampires can't enter a house without an invitation.

That old wives' tale.

You don't believe in fairy tales, do you?

I clamped my hands to my ears. He'd read my mind!

"Get out of my head!" I yelled, my voice echoing in the empty house. "I refuse you entry, Billy Scarecrow."

Billy Scarecrow? Is that what you call me? Oh, I like that. I really do.

He chuckled.

Thanks so much for the kind compliment.

Why wasn't he angry? Shouldn't he be seething with frustration by now?

It's very reassuring, isn't it, the thought that you can shut me out. Unfortunately for you, it's a complete myth.

"I don't believe you," I retorted. "I *refuse* to believe you!"

You should. Think about the other myths about my kind. We can't go outside in broad daylight, they say. Well, you already know that's not true.

A chill ran down my spine. He was right. The first time I saw him, it was late afternoon. The sun had been slowly sinking over the horizon but it was still shining brightly. And he had been able to stand there completely unaffected.

There you go. You know I'm right. Oh, I don't like direct sunlight. It plays havoc with my complexion.

That's the reason for the hat and coat. But turn me to ash? Make me catch fire? Forget it. It takes more than that to kill a vampire.

He flicked out a forked, serpent-like tongue and ran it down the glass in slow, meandering zig-zag patterns. Then he laughed. A sing song warning rang out in my head.

I'm coming to get you.

"No." I almost croaked the word, my throat was so tight and dry with fright. I ran to the window and drew the curtains so I didn't have to look at that leering, sinister face. Then I waited. A couple of minutes had gone by when the TV boomed behind me. I spun round. It had come on by itself. It was as if an invisible hand was flicking through the channels. Suddenly, the dizzy procession of images came to an abrupt halt and there he was again, the monster Billy Scarecrow.

"That's impossible," I murmured.

Instantly, his voice seeped out of the sound system.

"It's impossible," he sang, "teach a hunter not to feed, it's just impossible."

I was backing away, feeling behind me for the door when a new sound erupted behind me. It was the drip of the kitchen tap. I turned to see thick, black, tar-like slime oozing out of the tap and clucking into the sink. What was wrong with me? Why was I just standing gawping? There was something I could do. I had to phone my parents. Snatching my mobile from the table, I scrolled down to their number and pressed call. To my horror, it was his voice I heard next, the man in the fedora hat.

"Now really," he said, "did you think it was going to be that easy?"

There I stood in the kitchen doorway, transfixed by the sight of the bubbling, steaming slime that was filling the sink to the brim. As I watched, mesmerized by the thick, gelatinous substance, it started to transform itself into something recognizably human-like in form. The tar figure writhed and twisted, stretched and grew until Billy Scarecrow stood before me. For a moment or two he rocked back and forth, tensed and coiled like a predator, then he sprang to the floor and straightened himself until he towered above me.

Honey, I'm home!

He reached out a hand and I flinched at his touch. But I didn't move. I couldn't. My feet were glued to the spot.

Say goodbye to all this. You're coming with me.

His fingers rested on my shirt. I could feel his frosty touch through the fabric. Very slowly, his claw-like nails closed, twisting the cotton and drawing me closer. He breathed into my face. I felt the icy vapour stealing into my nostrils. It was making me dizzy.

Follow me out to the van.

By then, I was barely conscious. I was vaguely aware of my feet travelling down the hallway to the door. I sensed the door opening. Did he do that or did I? Then I was moving along the garden path towards the black van. There was at least one more of the creatures inside. I could make out the silhouetted outline of the driver at the wheel and I was fairly sure that there was somebody else in the back waiting, waiting for me. I wanted to cry for help but the word froze in my throat. I could no more have shouted out at that moment than I could fly.

That's right, in you get.

My mind was no longer my own. At his command, I reached for the side of the door. That's when the world exploded into blood and violence. A primal shriek of anguish erupted around me. Simultaneously, I felt the glacial sting of cold air on my face. The spell was broken. Disoriented, I looked around. Billy Scarecrow was reeling backwards, a crossbow bolt embedded in his throat. There was no blood but that didn't make the moment any less terrifying. A second vampire, the driver, was screeching her hatred at somebody behind me. I heard the newcomer's footsteps approaching, thudding on the pavement.

Get me out of here! The pain!

Billy Scarecrow was pleading for help. A sense of relief flooded through me as I saw the seemingly all-powerful monster reduced to a whimpering victim. I watched as he half-climbed, half-fell into the passenger seat of the black van. The engine roared and the vehicle leapt forward, accelerating violently as it gunned down the road. A second crossbow bolt, probably aimed at the tyres, clattered against the wheel rim and spun away. The van screamed round the corner and was swallowed by the London night.

I finally snapped out of my hypnotic dream-state and found my voice. Turning, I saw a tall, black woman, her dread-locked hair tied back by a maroon band.

"Looks like I arrived just in time," she said, a hint of breathlessness in her voice.

"Who are you?" I asked, utterly bewildered by the turn of events.

"I'm Elysia," she answered. "It means Heaven."

"But how…why…?"

I'm not even sure I knew what I wanted to ask. Elysia cut me off in mid-babble.

"My name's Elysia James," she said. "I have a mission. I kill vampires."

I nodded dumbly, as if it was the kind of thing you hear every day.

"But he seemed so powerful," I croaked, "then you…"

"They're as powerful as you allow them to be," Elysia interrupted. "If you let them play their mind games, you're dead meat. You have to shut them out. You have to move fast and hit hard."

She made it sound so simple.

"I won't be able to do this alone," she continued. "You'll have to come with me."

I held up my hands in protest. "Oh no. You can't be serious."

"I'm deadly serious," Elysia retorted. She turned her head, gazing in the direction the black van had sped. "If we don't kill the nest tonight, they'll be back for you. Is that what you want?"

I shook my head and followed her meekly to her motorbike, a Yamaha 750. She'd saved my life. How could I turn her down?

"There's a helmet in the top box," she said, pulling on her own skid lid. "I managed to put a tracking device on the van's chassis." She slapped a small electrical gizmo in my hand. "This reader unit will tell us which way they're going. Tap me on the shoulder to tell me which way to go. Can you do that?"

I nodded.

"Good," Elysia said. "Now sit tight, I won't be stopping for any red lights."

"What about the police?"

"Do you really think they're going to catch me on this?"

It was no idle boast. She opened the throttle and roared off down the road. I left my stomach a few hundred yards behind me. Recovering from the burst of acceleration, I concentrated on the task in hand. I'd been out on my uncle's bike so I knew the score. Hold tight, lean with the rider. We swept through the streets, weaving in and out of the late rush-hour traffic. My heart was thudding. What had I got myself into?

Then another thought struck me. What were Mum and Dad going to think when they walked into the empty house? For a moment, I saw through their eyes. They would see the smashed dish on the floor, the pasta splashed up the wall. They were bound to be out of their minds with worry. But what could I do? I clung on and kept my eye on the tracking device. I guided her ever closer to our target. It wasn't long before I realised where we were headed. We were less than a mile from Coogan's Row, the place where it had all begun.

The district where the Flea Market was held every Sunday was uncannily quiet as we approached. Elysia had slowed to walking space and the Yamaha idled along. I noticed that she was glancing left and

right, peering down each of the alleys that branched
off the main through road. I soon saw why. At the far
end of one such alley a police car was parked and
the officers were leaning against it talking. Elysia
stopped the bike and hoisted it onto its stand.

"Is that where Katie Swallow disappeared?" I
asked.

Elysia nodded. "And this is where we'll find her
abductors."

"But the police have searched the warehouses," I
protested.

Elysia took the tracking device from me.

"One problem," she said, "they didn't go deep
enough."

I didn't like the sound of that. My heart was
slamming as I followed her to a huge building over
to our left. The date of its construction was marked
out in brick: 1858.

"You mean they're in there?" I asked, my mouth so
dry with fright the question came out as a hoarse
whisper.

Elysia nodded. "With any luck, so is young Katie.
It's the fourth day. I just hope they haven't drained
her yet."

"Drained her?"

"They're bound to have fed," Elysia said, "but a
healthy prey can usually last a nest this size a week.
They came for you as her replacement when she…"

"Yes," I said, interrupting, "I get the picture. But
what have you brought me along for? I don't know
what to do."

Elysia unstrapped something that looked like a
fishing rod holder from the bike. It was made of blue

canvas. She unclipped the cover and showed me a quiver of crossbow bolts.

"I have to puncture each vampire's heart or brain with one of these," she said. "I'm very good at what I do, but there's no room for error." She showed me how the crossbow worked. You had to crank it back with a lever to give it enough force to penetrate bone and muscle. "I wouldn't be able to load it fast enough on my own." She grimaced. "My usual partner has gone missing. I think the goons may have got her."

"Goons?" I asked.

"Our word for the vampires," she explained. She tossed me the quiver. "All you have to do is hand me a bolt when I ask for one. Are you ready?"

I answered honestly. "No."

Elysia rested a hand on my shoulder. "I know exactly how you're feeling. The first time I went after a nest, I was trembling like a leaf. Just remember, they want to feed on you. They wouldn't hesitate to kill your parents too. "

"I'll do it," I told her. "Do you think we can kill them all?"

"I've got to make a kill every time," Elysia answered. "There are eight in goons in this nest. I've got exactly eight bolts left."

"Are you really that good?" I asked, remembering what she'd said.

"My name means Heaven," Elysia said, by way of an answer. "I plan to give them Hell."

It was about the best answer she could have given. It was confident, single-minded. She edged into the cavernous warehouse ahead of me. With a practised eye, she located the cast-iron cover that would admit us into the bowels of the building. Easing it off, she led the way down the steel ladder. It wasn't long before we were in pitch darkness. She pulled out a flashlight and started to explore the gloom.

"Can you smell that?" she whispered. "They're close."

It was a peaty smell, like damp earth.

"They fill their coffins with soil," Elysia explained. "They sleep with it smeared over their skin. It acts as a protection against any beams of light that find their way inside."

"That vampire said sunlight doesn't destroy them," I objected.

"He was telling the truth," Elysia confirmed, "but it can blister their flesh." She chuckled. "Believe me, it spoils their beauty sleep."

She broke off in mid-explanation.

"What is it?" I hissed.

She pressed a finger to her lips and handed me the flashlight. "There."

I could see it. One of the goons had just reared up out of its coffin. Its eyes, colourless in daylight, glittered silver in the dark. Elysia shot the crossbow. The bolt buried itself into the creature's chest. In less than two minutes she had discovered and destroyed four more of the things, annihilating them as they slept. But where were the last three? We crept forward. If Elysia was scared, she didn't show it.

"There!" she cried.

I slapped the next bolt into her palm. This time the goon was almost on top of her before she could send the bolt thumping into its eye socket. Like the others, the monster dissolved into ash. Two left. The search for the surviving pair took us deep, deep into the heart of darkness. Where were they? I was just reaching out to tug Elysia's sleeve and ask what we were going to do, when the seventh vampire sprang from the murk, knocking Elysia off her feet. The fall winded her and she lay writhing beneath the goon, desperately pushing its deadly fangs away from her throat. I scrambled after the crossbow.

"Use the lever," Elysia yelled. "Crank it back."

My hands were clammy with sweat. The first time I tried to low the bolt, the mechanism sprang back.

"I'm not strong enough," I cried.

"Do it!" Elysia screamed.

The second time, I drew it back in a single, even movement, the way I'd seen Elysia do it. With frantic, fumbling fingers, I shoved the bolt into the slot and released the traction. The bolt flew true and embedded itself into the back of the goon's skull. It showered Elysia with ash.

"Not bad," she chuckled, scrambling to her feet. "for a beginner."

But there was no time to exchange banter. There was still one vampire lurking in the shadows. I knew which one. It was the monster that had invaded my home. The thought made my heart turn to stone. Elysia had just started cranking back the crossbow wire when I heard something. I caught Elysia's stare. She'd heard it too. She mouthed a single word: *Katie.* We followed the sobs. Finally, I picked out her face. Her mouth was gagged, her eyes bulging. She was terribly pale but she was alive. She was trying to tell us something. I reached for the gag but she shook her head and trained her eyes on the darkness behind us. What was she trying to say? Then I understood.

Elysia spin round, but too late. The goon that had attacked me in my own home felled her with a vicious back-handed slap. The crossbow flew from her hand. This time there was no way I could reach it. The vampire was blocking my way. He gazed down with terrible satisfaction at the senseless form of Elysia. His sneering voice filtered into my thoughts.

I think we've got unfinished business.

He approached slowly, revelling in the terror he saw in my eyes.

Now it ends.

But, for the second time that evening, the monster's triumph turned to anguished defeat. This time, the bolt that struck him sank deep into his heart. I turned, bewildered by the turn of events. A familiar figure stepped out of the shadows carrying the crossbow that had spun from Elysia's grasp. It was the untidy, little woman I had met in the Flea Market.

"I've been searching for Katie," she explained. "I got lost in the labyrinth of tunnels. Looks like I rediscovered my sense of direction just in time."

Elysia was stirring. She saw Sally and started to roar with laughter. Sally winked at her.

"We did it," I murmured, hardly able to believe it. "We won."

Elysia ran her hand over her hair and smiled. "Yes, we won."

"This is fantastic," I cried. "I want to do what you do. I want to be a slayer."

Sally shook her head.

"No," she said, "you don't. You have been with us for a few hours. I've been at war with the goons for thirty years. You have no idea what the slayer's life like. We've got no home, no family, no roots. Our only home is the struggle. You don't understand the despair of the slayer."

I didn't get a chance to ask for a fuller explanation. There was a hiss behind us and Sally's face drained of blood. Elysia and I spun round. Immediately, we understood the transformation in her face. It was Katie. Her eyes were blazing scarlet and her teeth had mutated into fangs. The goons had turned her.

"We're too late," Sally groaned.

"What does that mean?" I demanded. "How do we help her?"

She failed to meet my eye.

"We don't," she said. "It's too late for that. All we can do is put her out of her misery and prevent her infecting others."

I saw her reach for one of the bolts lying in the heap of ash. In that moment I understood the despair of the slayer.

DARK SPACES

BY ALAN GIBBONS

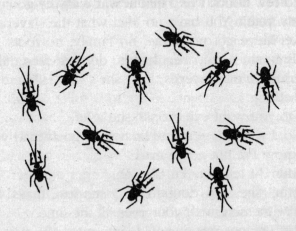

1

Sometimes I think I'm going mad. Not just a little bit bonkers. We're talking eye-popping, spit-dribbling, talking-in-tongues CRRR-AAZZY! It's the floaters, you see. You know what I mean, these little black spots that drift around the edges of your vision. It's as if there's something there, just out of sight, trying to push itself into view. I find myself turning my head, trying to see what this weird thing is that's bugging me. Then I notice somebody, Mum, Dad, my kid sister, one of the teachers, watching me and I stop. I mean, I'm making myself look like some kind of weirdo, twitching and blinking like that all the time. Mum's noticed. She would. I'm sitting at the kitchen table, covering first one eye then the other with my hand when she walks in.

'What's the matter with you?' she asks.

'Nothing.'

'Don't come that with me. Is it your eyes?'

Yes mum, it's my eyes. It's not the dancing darkness, the crawling madness, it's my eyes.

'It's nothing,' I say.

'Let me see.'

Now she's got her hands on my face. She's peering into my eyes like she's Dr Hibberd or something.

'Do you want eye drops?' she asks.

No, I want these stupid floaters to go away. I want to know I'm not going mad.

'Mum,' I tell her. 'I'm all right.'

'Mm,' she says doubtfully. 'I suppose that's why you're messing with your eyes all the time.'

But I'm not messing with my eyes. My eyes are messing with *me*. The floaters are doing it. They're even messing with my head. Finally, I tell her.

'I get these floaters.'

She breathes a sigh of relief.

'Oh, is that all? Everybody gets them sometime. They're harmless.'

That's what I thought- until last night.

I was sitting up in bed reading as usual. That's when the floaters came. I did what I always do, trying to blink them away or cupping a hand over my eye, Long John Silver style. There was a time that worked. Not any more. The floaters just carried on flickering away at the margins of my vision. But they weren't satisfied with just flickering. Something was happening. The floaters were changing, no, not changing, worse than that, *growing*. That's it, they were growing stuff, tiny feelers for starters. The tiny black dots looked different somehow, kind of....furry. I tried to concentrate on them but every time I tried to bring the things into focus they shrank back. I wasn't imagining it. I know what I saw, and what I saw were feelers, legs.

All day I've been thinking about the things, wondering what they are and how they can be growing. It's got so I don't want to go to bed tonight. That's when they come out, when I'm tired, or maybe it's just when they've got me on my own. Then they won't be blinked away or covered up or ignored. Then they change and grow.

'Bedtime in a quarter of an hour,' Mum says.

I've got to think of something to put it off. I pull out a notepad and start scribbling. It's like I'm in school doing one of those *My Life* things:

My name is Joe Kelly. I'm twelve. I live with my mum and dad and my pain in the neck sister Laura. I live at 15, Smith Grove. I go to Ridgemount High School.

I need to tell myself all this. It's as if the floaters are going to start nibbling away the basic facts of my life. Honestly, I'm going mad. But I won't let the floaters win.

An hour later, up in my room, I'm not so sure. There's something else about the floaters, something I didn't really notice until now. In a way, this is the most disturbing thing of the lot. They aren't in my eye at all. The things my mum is talking about, they're inside your eyeball, swimming round in the liquid or whatever's in there, all that eye-gunge. But these floaters, they're different. They're outside me, trying to get in. They're not just little bits of slime inside my eye, they're wriggling, black creatures and they're alive.

OK, OK, I'm really losing it here. I sound like Dr flipping Frankenstein. *They're alive! They're alive!* What am I talking about? Little black creatures, I'll be screaming about the wardrobe monster next! I daren't tell Mum and Dad. They'd be booking an appointment with the child psychologist. Hey doc, feel this kid's funny bumps. No, I've got to get a grip.

I'm Joe Kelly.
I'm twelve.
I'm not mad.

Sure about that?

I wake up in the middle of the night. There's a streetlamp outside my window. The sodium glare picks out shadows in the corner of my room. That's when I see them, the floaters. They're not floating at the fringe of my vision anymore. They're scuttling across the floor like bugs. Is that what they are, bugs? I turn on my light. That'll do the trick. Bugs always run from the light. I sit there grinning in triumph. Way to go Joe Kelly, world's most awesome bug-hunter!

Only I haven't got rid of them. There's one now, the size of a five pence coin. There's another. What are they? I squeeze my eyes shut. There was a time that worked. If I can't see you, you aren't there. But that was when they first appeared, when I thought they were just specks in my eye. I don't believe that anymore. These things, they've got a life of their own. I sit watching them, wondering what they want.

Then I make a decision. If you're bugs you can be swatted, squished. You can be turned into ex-bugs. Right, you've had it. I grab a Games Workshop catalogue and roll it up really tight. Bug-hunter armed.

Bug-squisher in hand, I swing my legs out of bed and advance on the scuttering black shapes. I'll have you now. Mess with Joe Kelly, will you? Well, the penalty is death.

Suddenly I'm swatting and beating at them for all I'm worth. I 'm sure I got them but they don't move or flinch, and they certainly don't squish. What are these things? Then I do something really gross. I reach out and *touch* one. Now I know why they don't squish. Whatever they are, they're not bugs. They're not made of bug stuff. In fact, they're not made of stuff at all. My finger goes right through, as if they're made of black gas, or shadow or something.

I do it again, just to make sure, poking and prodding like my life depends on it. I try to trap one of those legs, those feelers with my thumbnail but they're not solid either. That does it. I fly back to bed, tucking my legs under me and trapping the bedclothes round me, like that'll keep the things away.

I sit there for ages, trying to stare the floaters down. They cluster in the corner, half in and half out of the shadows, the dark spaces, staring back at me. Staring without eyes, how do you figure that?

That's how an hour goes, more, until I fall asleep, exhausted.

2

Sometimes I *know* I'm going mad. When I woke up this morning I was so happy. The sun was shining. The breeze was riffling the curtains. Life was good. Then I remembered the floaters. Instinctively I looked in the corner. That's when I knew I was going mad. The floaters, they'd eaten a hole in the skirting board. OK, rewind. Stop. Run that by me again. No, it sounds just as mad but it was true. There was a hole, the size of my fist. The dark spaces had come together to form a single, black, empty hole.

I'm sitting looking at it now. I've thought about it all day at school. There's something funny about it, this hole, something really weird. Then I've got it. This hole, there are no splinters of wood, no fragments of plaster, no wires, no specks of dust, nothing. You can't see anything, anything at all. The hole is black and the blackness goes on forever. I'm still staring at the hole when Mum knocks on the door.

'Are you all right?' she asks, poking her head round the door.

'Of course. Why?'

'It's not like you to sit up in your room on your own like this.'

I don't even turn to look at her. I just keep staring at the hole.

'What are you looking at?' she asks.

For a moment I feel excited.

'Do you see anything?'

'No. Like what?'

I shrug my shoulders. That confirms it. I'm the only one who can see the hole, same way I'm the only one who can see the floaters.

'Come downstairs and watch a bit of TV,' Mum says.

I can tell she's worried.

I didn't want to go to bed, but I'm here now. The hole's here too, and it's bigger, the size of two fists. I can see the floaters swarming all around the edges, nibbling away, opening the hole.

Wider.

Wider.

I make my mind up. I've got to do something. Heart thudding, I cross the floor and kneel down. Then I flatten my face to the floor, bringing my eyes level with the hole. All I see is the endless dark.

The floaters stop nibbling. It is as though they sense my interest. Maybe it's what they want, my attention. Bit by bit, they draw back from the hole, making a circle round it. Go on, they're telling me, take a look if you want to. There's nothing else for it. I reach out. I can see my fingers shaking. What if there's something there? What if it's like Indiana Jones? What if my arms get covered in bugs?

Black bugs made of shadow-stuff.

My fingertips are entering the hole. I hold my breath, suck it deep inside my chest. My fingertips move inside. There's nothing. It isn't hot. It isn't cold. There's nothing to touch, nothing at all. That's what the hole is, a nothing place. My hand's all the way in now.

In the nothing place.

An hour later, maybe more, I'm lying awake in bed. I'm breathing. The world is breathing too. That's all the sound there is, me and the world breathing. The hole doesn't breathe. The hole doesn't do anything.

It just is.

It's the nothing place.

Unable to sleep, I sit up. The floaters are back at work. The hole is the size of a dinner plate. The floaters are working patiently. They're like little, tiny robots. They work mechanically, reducing my room to blackness.

Then I notice something. They've changed again. In addition to the feelers, the squirmy, little leg things, they've got pincers. They're not bugs anymore. They're crabs. That's it exactly. They used to be nothing-bugs, now they're nothing-crabs.

I say my life story out loud:

My name is Joe Kelly. I'm twelve years old. I live with my mum and dad and my pain in the neck sister, Laura...

Then I freeze. What's the matter with me? I can't remember the rest. I stare at the floaters. It's you, isn't it? You're eating my life!

Finally I get it back. I remember:

I live at 15, Smith Grove. I go to Ridgemount High School.

I do a little dance in triumph. Thought you had me, didn't you? Well, think again, floaters.

You're just nothing-bugs.

You're just nothing-crabs.
You're nothing.

But I'm wrong.

There's more than nothingness in the hole. There's a world beyond. How do I know? It's raining through there. That's right, I can hear it, there's cold, driving rain in there. Here, in this world, it is a fine, dry night. Through there, in the floaters' world, there's a storm.

I go over to the hole. This time, when I reach out, my fingers don't shake quite so much, at least not to start with. I shove my hand in.

Up to the wrist.

Up to the freckles on my forearm.

Up to the elbow.

That's when I feel the rain. It's cold, like rain in this world. It feels like tiny needles, like rain in this world. But when I pull my hand back out I know the rain doesn't come from this world.

How do I know?

Because the rain is black.

When I leave for school the next morning the hole is the size of a plate. It's big enough to get your head inside. Only I don't put my head inside. I shiver at the thought. All day at school it's there, the plate-sized black hole. It seems to blot out everything else: my friends, the teachers, even the sun itself. No matter how hard I try, I can't think of anything but the hole. How big is it? Is it still raining in there? Am I going mad?

But when I get home I don't run upstairs to check. Now that I'm close, now that I'm thirteen stairs and ten paces from my room, I'll do anything to stay away. Twice Mum asks me to put my schoolbag in my room. Each time I manage to ignore her. I just hang round downstairs. I watch TV. I squabble with Laura. I even do my homework on the kitchen table. Anything so I don't have to face the hole.

It's about half past eight when I hear Mum's voice.

'Joe, get up these stairs this very minute.'

My skin prickles. Her voice is coming from upstairs.

'Joe.'

I reach the landing. Not just upstairs, she's in my room. Does that mean she can see it? I'm not alone. I'm not going mad.

'Come in here, please.'

I walk through the door.

'Would you like to explain this?'

It's not the hole. She's waving a library book around.

'It's three weeks overdue.'

'Sorry.'

'Just take it back tomorrow. And Joe…'

'Yes?'

'The fine is coming out of your pocket money.'

She leaves the room, shutting the door behind her. That's when I see the hole. It's as big as I am. Worse, it's in the shape of a human figure. Mine.

I stand a few steps from the hole. I plant my feet slightly apart, the way the feet of the black figure are placed. I reach out my arms until they match the figure. It's my height, my build. Everything matches perfectly.

'What do you want?' I ask.

The black hole doesn't answer. I didn't really expect it to. It's a hole. I'm still standing staring at the black figure, the strange shadow-me, when the bedroom door opens behind me.

'Put these clothes away Joe,' Mum says. 'Don't crease them. I've only just ironed them.'

Then her voice trails away.

'What are you doing?'

I know she can't see the hole so there's no point asking her.

'Nothing.'

I catch her reflection. Her mouth moves as if she's going to say something. She doesn't. As soon as I'm alone again I sit on the end of the bed staring straight ahead. The black, empty face of the shadow-me stares back. It's eyeless like the nothing-crabs but it is watching. I can feel it.

'You're waiting for me, aren't you?'

Funny how *yes* can be silent, wordless but definitely there.

The hole can wait all it wants. At bedtime I take off my clothes and curl up under the bedclothes. I lie watching my alarm clock, waiting for the minutes to change. I know I won't sleep. Time crawls by. Every minute seems to last an hour but I keep my eyes fixed on the red numerals. Anything is better than turning to face the shadow-me on the wall.

It's about two o'clock in the morning when I hear the rain, the black rain in the place beyond the hole. There is a black, magnetic force oozing from the place beyond, tugging at me, telling me to turn around.

Suddenly it is as though the silent words have

barbed ends and they are sticking in my flesh. They're yanking my skin, tugging at me, trying to twist me round.

But I won't.

'You can't make me!'

There, I've done it. I've said it out loud. I expect Mum and Dad to come and ask what's wrong. But they don't hear. That seems to encourage the hole. The black rain starts again. Then there is the rush of wind, black wind. But it isn't like any wind I've ever felt. It starts at the wall and rushes into the world beyond, whipping and howling and daring me to follow.

That's what it's about. That's what it's all about. The dark spaces want me.

The next day it isn't just Mum and Dad who are worried. Now everybody is asking if I'm all right.

'You look tired,' they say.

'Your eyes are bloodshot.'

'You look awful.'

Thanks. Thanks a lot.

Well, you'd be tired if you had dark spaces in your room. Try it, go on, just try lying there night after night, not daring to turn round. Try lying on your side with your eyes glued to your alarm clock all night.

Try it.

Try it!

Try it!

Who am I talking to? Oh, that's it. I am going mad. The dark spaces are inside my head, turning my brain to mush.

I walk home like a zombie, grunt a hello to Mum, Dad and Laura and walk upstairs. I don't even try to stay away from my room tonight. To my surprise nothing has changed. The dark figure is still there, the shadow-me, feet slightly apart, arms reaching out at its side. But that's it. There are no floaters, no nothing-bugs, no nothing-crabs. They've done their job. It's just me and my shadow-me.

I take up my position, a few steps from it. I plant my feet slightly apart. I reach out my arms and I face it, the dark space that is waiting for me. Then I say, very slowly, very deliberately:

My name is Joe Kelly. I'm....

The black rain starts. The black wind howls. They carry my thoughts away.

My name is Joe Kelly. I'm twelve. I live with...

The black rain hammers on the earth beyond the hole, in the dark spaces that are waiting for me. The black wind whips and tears and hollers.

My name is Joe Kelly. I'm twelve. I live with my mum and dad and my pain in the neck sister....

But the black rain is beating harder. It seems to have got inside my head. It prickles against the insides of my eyelids. It swirls in my throat.

My...sister....Laura.

No, that's not right. I'm losing it. The dark spaces are eating away at my words. I'm dissolving into the blackness.

I live at....

The black wind roars. It scours my brain, sighing inside my thoughts.

I live...

Suddenly I am just a few inches from the dark figure, the shadow-me.

'No, I didn't move.'

But I must have.

I live...

I...

Then I'm inside the shadow-me. Its edges cling to me. The black rain falls and the black wind roars.

The dark spaces have me.

3

In movies and stories people do this all the time. They go through wardrobes, portals, gateways. They visit other worlds, other dimensions. I know what to expect. Don't I? But I didn't expect *this*.

There are no talking animals, no fauns, no dwarves, no golden lions. There are no rivers, no forests, no hills. There are no glittering cities. There's no yellow brick road. There is...nothing. I'm in complete darkness. I'm standing alone in the black, drenching rain. All around me it's beating down, drumming against the earth. Only it isn't earth. It's like shale, ash. It seems to cling to my feet, black and gluey, sucking at my ankles. It would make it difficult to walk. That's if there was anywhere to walk *to*. But there isn't. There is nowhere to go. My eyes are adjusting now. For as far as the eye can see there is black, featureless earth stretching towards a black, featureless horizon. And above that?

Sky.

Black sky.

I'm in a nothing-land. I'm nowhere and, no matter

how hard I search, there is no way back. There is no wall, no hole, no shadow-me. There's nothing but the dark spaces.

Nothing.

Suddenly my eyes are stinging. I don't cry. Like they say, big boys don't cry. Not me. Not Joe Kelly.

My name is Joe Kelly. I'm twelve. I live....

A lump rises in my throat. I'm choking on my own sobs.

I live at 15, Smith Grove.

But I don't, do I? Not any more, maybe not ever again. Because there's no way home. It isn't like the Wizard of Oz. There are no ruby slippers. There are no magic words.

But there are words.

'I want to go home!'

There isn't even an echo in this place. The black, howling wind swallows my voice.

In the end I start walking. The direction doesn't matter, only the act of walking. I can't just stand there rubbing my eyes, being scared. Maybe there is no way back, but I have to try.

'You won't beat me!' I yell. From somewhere I've dragged up my last reserves of defiance. 'OK, so you got me here, but I'm going to get back, you just watch me.'

With that, I trudge forward through the clinging shale. It feels like I'm walking for hours. Still the rain falls. Still the wind howls. The dark spaces won't beat me.

The weird thing is I don't seem to tire at all. On and on I walk. But no matter how far I walk, nothing bothers me. I don't feel wet or cold or hungry. It is as though I'm stronger now, different. I've changed. Hey, maybe I'm the nothing-bug here. Maybe there's a shadow-me somewhere round here who's going to see a little Joe Kelly nothing-bug eating *his* wall. Wouldn't that be something?

'See, I told you you weren't going to beat me. Listen to this: **My name is Joe Kelly. I'm twelve years old. I live with my mum and dad and my pain in the neck sister, Laura.**'

Go on, go on talking.

'I live at 15, Smith Grove. I go to Ridgemount High School. *And I'm going home.*'

That makes me feel strong, angry, so I start yelling.

'I'm going home and you can't stop me.'

The rain starts to lessen. Don't tell me this is working.

'You…can't…stop…ME!'

The rain stops howling. There, there in the darkness, I can see it, the hole. I don't believe it. I'm going home. I'm Joe Kelly and I'm going home. There is hope. There is a way back. I start running. The hole seems to stretch out to meet me. It takes the shape of the shadow-me. I plant my feet slightly apart. I reach out my arms. I fall forward. When I open my eyes there's my room, my bed, my wall…and there's no hole any more. It's gone. The nightmare is over.

I did it.

I fought the dark spaces and I won.

Hey, meet Joe Kelly, King of the Ruby Slippers.

Then I hear something, like scuttering feet, lots of scuttering feet. I turn round. No, it can't be. Fear trickles down my spine. I'm just imagining it. Just listen to me world, I fought the dark and I won. Then I hear something else, like claws opening and closing. That's it, pincers. They are crunching and grinding. No, no way. But I know it's true. Behind me there is something black and eyeless watching me. But it is different somehow, more real, more dangerous. The nothing-crabs never made a noise before. They were just empty space, shadow stuff. How could they…?

That's when my insides start to melt. Oh God, no. No, I couldn't be that wrong. I couldn't have got it all completely wrong.

'No!'

'Joe, what's wrong?'

It's Mum's voice.

'Don't come in,' I yell.

She doesn't listen. I see her at the door, her and Dad and Laura.

'Get out,' I cry. 'Please.'

I hear the feet. I hear the pincers. I was such a fool. That shadow-me, it was the keyhole and I was the key. I opened the door and let in the dark. I let in….*that*.

I see the shadow of the nothing-crab, the body, the legs, the pincers. It isn't shadow-stuff any more. It's solid. It's real. It's *huge*. I was the key. I let it in.

I see my family staring with wide, horrified eyes. I hear their screams. They see it now.

I'm Joe Kelly.

I went into the dark spaces…

…and…

…Oh no, how can I say it….

I've brought something back.

HOME ALONE

BY ROBBIE GIBBONS

1

She was gorgeous. She had long, dark hair, pretty green eyes, a Hollywood smile. It was a shame that just below her colour portrait the word 'MISSING' was printed in bold, along with contact details and the promise of a reward if she was found alive. We were looking at a poster that had been pasted to a lamppost not far from our new house.

"Apparently she's the fifth one this month," Jay commented drily.

Great, I thought. Dad's decided to move us to Abductorsville!

It was our first week in the new neighbourhood, and me and my older brother Jay already hated it.

Neither of us had made any friends in our new school, the uniform was ugly, and now we've just found out that the area was prone to the occasional child disappearance. Just great!

"Best not to tell Dad," Jay said. "He worries too much as it is."

It's no wonder he worried. He hadn't been the same since Mum died. I nodded and we continued to walk, when I noticed Mr. Lynch staring from his usual speck. Oh, I forgot to mention. If things weren't bad enough we also lived in a street full of nosey, stuck-up pensioners who apparently viewed our arrival as an unbearable intrusion into their cosy, wrinkly little community.

"He's looking again," I mumbled.

Jay glanced over the road, where Mr. Lynch was peering at us disapprovingly from beneath a wide-brimmed straw hat. Only his head and shoulders were visible above his garden fence, which he had been in the process of painting for days with seemingly no progress. 'Mr. Lynch' wasn't his real name, of course. Jay had dubbed him so because he looked as if he belonged in a 1930's Lynch mob.

"Ignore him, the old fart," Jay said, gesturing in the old man's direction. If he noticed, Mr. Lynch registered no response, and merely continued to glare in silence.

As we reached the front door of our new house I glanced back over my shoulder to see if Mr. Lynch was still watching, but he had disappeared once more behind his half-painted fence. There was definitely something funny about our new neighbourhood. Everyone was creepy.

We burst through the front door with our usual ceremonious arrival. "We're home!" Jay declared, at the top of his lungs.

"I know," echoed Dad's voice from the kitchen. "Four o'clock sharp is when peace and quiet officially ends."

"So... what are we having to eat?" Jay asked.

"You tell me," Dad smiled. "You're the ones making it. If you're staying in the house alone you should at least cook for yourselves."

We responded with a simultaneous groan. Cooking was for parents. Tonight Dad had to go on some business trip in Wales, so me and Jay were on our own for the night.

"I'll be back about noon tomorrow," he assured us. "And don't forget to lock the doors before you go to bed."

As soon as he was out the door Jay and I exchanged a glance. "Takeaway?" I suggested.

"You bet," he said, already looking up the number for 'Pizza Hut' in the phonebook. "Oh and I've got a surprise for you later."

"What is it?"

"You'll see." He said it as an afterthought, but there was an impish glint in his eyes that told me he was planning something I wasn't going to enjoy.

As it turned out, I was right.

2

It was astonishing how different the house felt at night. I hadn't really noticed it until we were alone, but the place had undergone a rapid and sinister transformation. The darkness somehow causes a heightened sense of awareness. I found myself jumping at every sound, alarmed by every slight movement. It's stupid, I know, but at fourteen years of age I'm still afraid of the dark.

Jay knew it, which is why he insisted we turn all the lights off. After several minutes of being called a 'chicken' I had reluctantly accepted, and so here I was sat amidst a pile of empty pizza boxes in the hallway upstairs with an electric torch waiting for Jay to reveal his much anticipated 'surprise'.

After a few moments he appeared brandishing a flat, well-polished slab of hardwood.

"That's the surprise?" I asked quizzically, making no attempt to hide my disappointment.

Jay nodded, a mischievous smile painted on his lips. "It's a 'Ouija board'," he declared.

"What's a '*Wee-jah*' board?"

"I'll show you."

He placed the board flat in the centre of the floor. I looked at it closely. The surface of the wood was engraved with letters and numbers, and the edges were decorated with fanciful images of pyramids, moons, and other strange symbols. None of it made any sense to me, and Jay seemed to enjoy my confusion.

"What is it?" I asked.

"It's a game."

"Like... monopoly?"

Jay laughed. "No, Timmy. Not like monopoly."

"How do you play?"

Jay produced a small piece of wood from his pocket. "With this," he said, placing it in the centre of the board. I inspected the piece. It was pointed at the top with a curved edge at the bottom. In the centre a perfect hollow circle had been cut out so that you could see through the middle.

"What is it?" I asked.

"It's the pointer," Jay explained. "It's what we use to communicate."

"Who with?"

Jay's eyes lit up. "Spirits."

"As in ghosts?" I asked. It didn't surprise me. Since we were home alone I knew that whatever Jay's 'surprise' turned out to be it would inevitably boil down to another intricate plot to scare me.

"Exactly," he smiled. "It's a new house. We need to find out if it's haunted."

I believed in ghosts, but I knew full well that Jay didn't. My guess was that he was planning to wait for an appropriate moment to shout 'Boo!' and make me jump. I thought the whole 'Ouija board' thing was unnecessary, but on the other hand Jay had been known to go to extraordinary lengths to give me a fright. I decided to play along anyway, thinking 'what's the worst that could happen?'

It was a decision I would soon regret.

Jay sat down cross-legged on one side of the board and me on the other.

"Now, we both place two fingers of each hand lightly on the pointer, like this," he said, demonstrating as he spoke. "We ask a question, and then close our eyes and concentrate. If there are any spirits in the area, they'll make contact with us using the pointer."

He sounded as if he had memorised the

instructions. I looked at the board once more. It was geared towards a question/answer scenario, with the words YES and NO at the top, and the alphabet and numbers beneath for more complicated answers.

"So the pointer thing is meant to just move on its own?"

"With the direction of the spirits," Jay corrected.

I laughed at that. Of all the crazy schemes Jay had used to scare me, this took it to a new level.

He scowled at me. "Just close your eyes."

I still thought the whole thing was some kind of prank, but I obeyed regardless. After all, what's the worst that could happen? I didn't like closing my eyes though. For some reason it made me feel nervous.

Jay asked the first question. He spoke in a dull monotone and I found the seriousness in his voice almost comical. He sounded like he was trying to imitate Derren Brown or one of those other ghost guys from TV.

"Is there anyone here, apart from us?"

I kept my eyes closed and waited in silent anticipation. For a few awkward moments there was no response. After waiting patiently I decided this was stupid. Nothing was going to happen. Jay was just trying to scare me. I was about to open my eyes when a slight trembling beneath my fingers made me jump slightly. I kept my eyes scrunched shut and resisted the urge to tear my hands away, although I could feel my fingers begin to tremble slightly.

Again I waited, but nothing happened.

But I was sure I felt it move, had I imagined it?

No! There it was again, the faintest of trembles! This was followed up by a stronger movement, and another, until I could feel the pointer steadily sliding across the surface of the wood.

Jay's moving it, I thought. He's just trying to scare me.

But if he was, it was working.

When the pointer had stopped moving we both opened our eyes. It had landed over the word 'YES'.

"See," Jay said triumphantly. "There's someone else here. I knew this house was haunted."

"What now?" I asked, assuming a seemingly uninterested tone to feign bravery.

"Next question," He answered. "We've established contact now, so you can keep your eyes open."

Thank God for that, I thought. Once again we placed our fingers lightly on the wooden pointer and prepared for the next question.

"What is your name?" Jay asked, in the same slow voice as before.

The pointer moved again, more quickly this time. I didn't think it would be as scary with our eyes open, but I was wrong. There was something disturbing about the way the pointer glided seamlessly across the board. We watched wide-eyed as the slim piece of wood moved towards the letters and paused on each once in sequence. First it landed on the letter V, then after a moments hesitation moved across the board to the letter I. Next was C, then T... O... and R.

"VICTOR," Jay proclaimed. "The ghost is called Victor."

I was more convinced than ever that it was Jay

moving the pointer, but that didn't stop a cold shiver running down my spine.

Jay wasted no time in asking the next question. "What do you want?"

Again the pointer trembled into action. R... then E... V... E... N... G... and E.

REVENGE.

I'd had enough. This was getting ridiculous. I pulled my hands away and folded my arms in defiance. "I'm not playing!" I declared. "You're just trying to scare me!"

Jay looked at me, his face a mask of innocence. "No I'm not."

"Yes you are! You've been moving it all along. It's not funny anymore!"

"No I wasn't! I thought you were."

I opened his mouth to offer a response, but just then a sudden movement in the corner of my eye caught my attention. It was the pointer. Neither of us had our hands anywhere near the board.

"Did you see that?" Jay asked.

I had. The pointer had trembled, without either of us touching it. "It was you!" I accused him, more in hope than conviction.

Jay merely shook his head raised both his hands to prove his innocence. "My hands are right here. I never touched it." Just then, as if to prove his point, the pointer moved again. Both of us instinctively jumped back, and watched in horrified silence as it spontaneously whizzed across the surface of the board.

H, the pointer landed on. Then it suddenly shot over to I. It moved again, just as quickly, but I was too frozen in shock to follow it with my eyes. Eventually it came to rest motionless in the centre of the board where we had left it, as if nothing had happened.

I could scarcely believe my eyes. Part of me still wanted to believe that Jay was playing some sort of elaborate prank on me, but the look on his face told otherwise. He was just as shocked as I was.

"It moved on its own!" I croaked, shaking my head in disbelief. The pointer had moved too fast for me to read its message, however. "What did it say?" I asked.

"HIDE," Jay breathed. "It told us to HIDE."

Several things happened at that moment. The pointer flew across the room so fast that both of us jumped, there was a loud crashing noise from somewhere downstairs, and the light of the torch suddenly went out, leaving us submerged in blackness.

I instantly started to panic. I was terrified of the dark. My initial reaction was to reach over to where Jay had been sitting, but he was gone.

"Jay!" I shouted. "What's happening?" There was no response. Now I was in full panic mode.

"Jay!" I called again. No one answered, but I couldn't shake the feeling that I wasn't alone. I scrambled to my feet and started frantically searching for the light switch instead. After a few moments of fumbling blindly across the wall with my hands I found it, but my relief was short-lived. I flicked it back and forth several times but the hall remained pitch black.

"Jay!" I called for the third time. I could hear my own voice breaking in desperation.

A light suddenly came on right in front of me, illuminating a gaunt face just inches away from my own. I tried to scream, but a powerful hand cupped my mouth.

"Shhhh... it's me," Jay whispered. He was holding the torch, pointed upwards, beneath his chin, the way Dad used to do when he told ghost stories. It gave his face an eerie and frightening look.

I tore his hand away from my face. "You scared me!" I said angrily.

"Shhhh," Jay repeated, holding a finger to his lips and handing me my own torch. "I think there's someone downstairs."

We both remained silent. He was right. I remembered hearing a loud noise just before the light went out, and now as I listened more carefully I could clearly hear a muffled clamour coming from downstairs. We were not alone.

Suddenly I was struck with a terrifying thought. "What if it's...?"

Jay finished my sentence for me. "Victor!"

The noises downstairs were getting louder. This can't be happening, I thought. In my mind I was searching desperately for some kind of logical explanation for all this. But nothing could alleviate the knot of fear brooding in the pit of my stomach.

I crept towards the edge of the staircase and peered down into the gloom. Any doubts I had left disappeared. At the bottom of the stairs stood a hunched, shadowy figure. I couldn't see properly in the darkness, but it appeared to be looking right at me!

I felt naked, caught in the icy grip of its gaze. I finally had to admit to myself that this was no joke.

This was really happening. Suddenly I remembered the advice of the Ouija board.

"Hide!" I hissed.

We raced to Dad's room, slamming the door behind us. Our search for a place to hide became frenzied. Jay dived in the wardrobe and I threw myself to the floor and scrambled under Dad's bed. I immediately regretted this decision, however. There was only one door into Dad's room and the window was too small for me to climb through, as well as being on the second floor. Long story cut short: we had no means of escape.

My heart was racing. I tried to steady my breathing but found myself panting like a dog. Jay had dropped the torch outside, and I had to wait for my eyes to adjust to the darkness. I could hear loud footsteps as Victor started ascending the creaky wooden staircase.

Creak, creak.

I tried to replay it all in my head. How had we gotten into this mess? It was Jay! Him and his damn board! We had disturbed a spirit from its slumber and now it wanted revenge. Victor was coming for us!

Creak, creak.

I watched the door, praying for it to remain closed.

Creak, creak.

There was nothing left to do now but wait. The footsteps were louder now. Victor was upstairs!

I held my breath and waited, but the footsteps had stopped.

The silence was deafening. I listened intently, but could hear nothing apart from the hammering of my own heart. The last footsteps had been right outside, but now they had stopped. I was hit with the sick realisation that it must be standing right there on the other side of the door, waiting... *listening.*

To my horror the doorknob started to turn. I didn't want to watch, but found myself unable to tear my eyes away from the slow rotation of the handle. I shuffled backwards further under the bed and lay flat on my stomach, daring not even to breathe. With a soft whine the door began to creak open.

From underneath the bed I could only see the bottom few inches of the room. The door continued to swing inwards until it stood wide open and a pair of black, thick-soled, muddy boots appeared in the room. Did ghosts wear boots? It was an odd thing to think at such a desperate moment. The intruder took a few steps forward and stopped by the bed, his boots only inches away from my face. They were close enough for me to make out what appeared to be spackled blood stains. I had to clasp a hand over my mouth to stifle an instinctive gasp.

"Playing hide and seek are we?" Victor said in a menacingly playful voice. "I like games."

I watched as the boots moved slowly towards the other side of the room, landing with a heavy clunk upon each step. My relief that he was moving away from me was countered by the realisation that he was edging closer and closer to where Jay was hiding.

"Come out, come out, wherever you are."

It was really dusty under Dad's bed, and I found it hard to breathe. I could feel my nose start to tingle. Oh no, I thought. Please not now.

Victor was obviously enjoying himself now. W
each step he chimed. "Warmer? No? ...How abc
now?"

My nose was still tingling.

Don't sneeze, I told myself. Whatever you do,
don't sneeze.

But I couldn't hold it in any longer.

I sneezed.

I tried to muffle the sound by clasping both hands
over my face, but it did little good. The noise
seemed deafening.

Victor spun round. "Aha!"

I watched frozen as the blood-stained boots
moved back to the edge of the bed.

"Hmm... where could he be?"

Victor started to crouch down on one knee. This
was it, I thought. I couldn't see his face, but the reality
couldn't possibly be worse than how I envisioned it
in my mind. His decomposing face twisted into a sick,
undead smile. His yellow eyes sparkling with delight
at the fact that he had cornered his prey. I didn't want
to see him, so I closed my eyes and awaited whatever
fate Victor had in stall for me.

I expected to feel his icy claws grasp me at any
moment, but it never came. Instead I heard a scream
as Jay burst from his hiding place.

"Leave him alone!" he cried.

I opened my eyes to see a struggle ensuing
between the two of them. I crawled forward to get a
better look. That's when I saw the intruder's face. It
wasn't Victor. It wasn't a ghost at all. It was Mr. Lynch
from across the street! Of course, I thought. It wasn't
blood on his boots, it was paint! I cursed myself for

jumping to such superstitious conclusions, but essentially the situation hadn't changed. There was still an intruder in the house, ghost or no ghost, and evidently he didn't wish us well.

Jay had jumped onto Mr. Lynch' back, and was beating him around the head with both fists. The powerfully-built older man swung round and caught him with a blow to the head so hard it knocked him to the floor. Jay's eyes were closed and he appeared to be unconscious. Mr. Lynch grabbed his legs and dragged him into the hallway.

I didn't know what to do. During the struggle something small and silver had fallen off the bedside table and landed on the floor. It was Dad's mobile. I glanced through the open doorway, where Mr. Lynch was still dragging Jay away by his feet. Either he had forgotten about me or he was planning on coming back for me. Either way I had the initiative, for the moment at least. I grasped the mobile and punched in the first number that came to mind.

999.

As the ringing tone sounded I could hear commotion in the hallway. What now? I thought. Everything was happening so fast.

I could hear Mr. Lynch. "N...No! It can't be!"

Was he talking to himself? I crawled forward and risked a look into the hallway. Jay was still out cold. Mr. Lynch was talking to someone else.

"You're... d... dead! This can't be happening!"

I followed Mr. Lynch's gaze and what I saw next was simply beyond explanation. There was a young boy, about my age, standing in the hall with his arms outstretched. He had a pale complexion, and seemed almost to radiate in the darkness. His expression was peculiar, emotion-less, yet somehow full of malice and marked with an unmistakeably menacing intent.

"S...Stay back!" Mr. Lynch commanded.

His voice was quivering, and had lost all of its malevolence. He sounded like a child.

The boy took no notice, and continued to walk slowly towards him, reaching out with both hands. Mr. Lynch looked like he wanted to run, but remained frozen to the spot.

"No!" He cried. It was the last word he ever spoke. As the boy reached out to touch him he grasped his chest with one arm and began to gasp breathlessly. He was pale and sweating. With a final pathetic whimper he collapsed and lay motionless.

The young boy stood over his lifeless body, a grim smile on his lips. His expression eased and became peaceful. The last thing he did was look straight at me, but I wasn't scared. Something in his face let me know he meant me no harm. Then in the blink of an eye he was gone.

I was left in a speechless daze. My brain still hadn't quite processed what I had just witnessed. I was snapped out of the trance by the sound of the 999 man on the mobile phone, which I still held dumbly to my ear.

"Hello," he was saying. "Is anybody there?"

I could only muster two words.

"He's dead," I breathed.

3

The next day was chaos. The police had arrived to investigate the 999 call to find a corpse in a house with two children alone. Neither of us were able to offer any solid explanation, apart from a disjointed story about ghosts. Naturally, they thought we were crazy, and we were treated as prime suspects. Matters got worse when Dad arrived home. He was furious, sick with worry too, and had no more luck than the police when he tried to question us.

An investigation ensued, and the police discovered evidence of forced entry though the back door. Apparently Mr. Lynch had died of a heart attack. That was a relief; At least we weren't in the frame for murder.

With no means of identifying the old man, the police had searched his house. That was when the case took a dramatic turn for the worse. In Mr. Lynch' basement, the bodies of five local children were found. We were spared the details of how they were killed. To be honest, I didn't want to know.

After that it was considered case closed. However bizarre it may have sounded at first, everything about my story added up. Well, apart from the young boy who had vanished into thin air. However, Dad did offer some explanation whilst reading the newspaper report a few days later.

"Hmm, that's odd," he commented, giving me a strange look.

"What is?" I asked.

"Once of the victims was the kid who lived in this very house before we moved in." He dropped the newspaper in front of me so that I could see for myself. "His name was Victor Jones."

The House of Fun

By Alan Gibbons

Jack was the one who called it the House of Fun. That Spring of 1982, the song was number one in the charts. Jack loved Suggs and Madness. He could do a good impression of Suggsy and an even better impression of the band's silly walk. Jack had the same sense of humour. The bet was his idea. The three of us, Jack, Smiler and me would stay in the old, abandoned house all night. It seemed like a good idea at first. It turned out to be the worst decision of our lives.

It took some planning. The first problem was how to put our parents off the scent. We were only twelve and they weren't about to OK a mad adventure like that. So we roped in another of our mates, Andy. He was the cautious type. No way would he join in our plan; he liked his bed too much. But he agreed to cover for us. He told all our parents we were having a sleepover at his house. My Mum and Dad swallowed it hook, line and sinker. That was how we solved our second problem; how to get all the stuff we needed for an overnight stay out of our houses. Andy said his house was short of spare beds so my parents picked up everybody's sleeping bags and took them to Andy's in the car.

About ten o'clock that Friday night, we left Andy's and set off up the hill to Palatine House. That's the proper name for the place we called the House of Fun. We'd been there often enough but never after dark, never at night. Things seem different then. The gloom makes everything creepier. In those days, you took a long, winding gravel path to Palatine House. The Lime Tree estate hadn't been built yet. There was no lighting. The place had been abandoned for years. The old Victorian gas lamps remained, but they had long since fallen into disuse. They stood as a rusting reminder of the House's glory years when it belonged to the Rathmore family. There were stories about the Rathmores. Andy reckoned that old man Rathmore murdered his entire family one night a hundred years ago. We used to tell him he had an over-active imagination. We should have listened to him.

Shouldering our sleeping backs, we carried on up the hill. It was windy that night. The gusts swirled and snapped around us. The gorse nodded as we passed, as if it knew something but wasn't letting on.

At one point, an owl screeched in the woods. Smiler stopped dead.

"What was that?" he asked, wide-eyed.

"Nothing," Jack told him, "just a vampire feeding."

"Yeah, very funny," Smiler snorted, "hah, hah, ow…"

He'd been too distracted by the sound of the owl and walked straight into a gorse bush. Jack and I burst out laughing. Struggling out of the bushes, Smiler scowled.

"It's not funny," he snapped. "Look at me, I'm scratched to bits. I feel like going home."

"Chicken," Jack mocked and started clucking at Smiler.

We called Liam Hughes Smiler because he was so serious. The nickname's meant to be ironic, or do I mean sarcastic?

"Chicken yourself," Smiler grumbled, stamping off down the path.

"Oh, don't go off in a huff," I said. "What are you going to say to your parents? You can't just turn up at half past ten. Besides, you'll get us in trouble. Come on, Smiler, we didn't mean to tease."

"Yeah, come back," Jack said. "We were having a laugh, OK?"

Smiler turned and looked at me before shifting his gaze to Jack.

"I'm sorry," Jack said, not very convincingly. " Now, can we go? I'm getting cold."

For April, it was bitterly cold. The icy wind boomed over the hillside, penetrating our clothes. Smiler nodded and trudged back in our direction. Then, strung out across the path, we carried on towards the House of Fun. Soon, we arrived at the ancient, rusted gates. You could make out the Rathmore family crest, even at night. It's a raven, its wings at full stretch, its head turned as if to examine any passing stranger. You still see it in a few places across town.

"The bird of death," Jack said.

"Knock it off," I told him. "Smiler's scared enough as it is."

"I am not scared!" Smiler protested. Then, dropping his voice, he asked: "Why's it the bird of death?"

"Something to do with the Vikings, I think," Jack said.

With that, he shoved open the iron gates. So rusted were the hinges, they only opened so far. They creaked as we stepped through the gap. We loved exploring the gardens on our visits to the House of Fun. It was full of surprises. There was a crumbling gazebo down by the lake. Here and there amid the tangled undergrowth that was once a well-tended garden, you would find various statues, some of them so worn you could barely recognize what they were meant to be. Somehow, at night, everything looked more sinister. Shadows hinted at a hidden menace. The statues seemed to crouch, waiting to leap out at us.

"I don't think this is such a good idea," Smiler said, gazing around. "My Dad says the crazies come out at night."

"Your Dad's as big a wimp as you are," Jack observed.

Smiler didn't answer, but he looked hurt. As usual, I tried to referee between them.

"It's just the dark playing tricks," I said. "There's nothing to worry about."

Nothing to worry about. If only I'd known.

"Hey, there it is," Jack announced, pointing across the broad, paved plateau at the far side of the garden.

There it was, the House of Fun. Instinctively, I allowed my gaze to travel up to the attic room at the top of the house. I frowned. Why hadn't I noticed this before? I counted the floors up to the attic. It jutted out of the roof just above the third floor.

"How many floors have we explored?" I asked.

Jack answered. "Three, why?"

"So why have we never found a way into that attic?" I asked.

Jack made a show of counting the floors.

"Hey, you're right," he said. "Cool, there must be a hidden room. Let's be the first to find the way in."

"You're kidding right?" Smiler said. "I hope you're not planning to go looking for it in the dark."

"Oh, come on," Jack said, striding on ahead. "Where's your sense of adventure?"

I met Smiler's eyes. Sense of adventure? He didn't have one. It had been murder trying to persuade him to join in the bet. Smiler thought Andy had the right idea, staying home tucked up in his own warm bed. At that moment Smiler must have wished he'd been as strong-willed as Andy was.

"Hurry up, you two," Jack said, starting to jog towards the front door. "Let's get inside before all the ghosts turn in for the night."

Funny guy. Smiler and I plodded after him. By then, I was starting to think Smiler had the right idea. The later it got, the more I wanted to turn round and go home. Neither of us did, of course. We ended up following Jack inside like a pair of sheep. It wasn't a bit like our previous visits. Even Jack seemed overawed by the inside of the House of Fun at night. The high, vaulted ceiling soared to such heights it was lost in the murk. The heavy velvet curtains hung in tatters at the windows. They reminded me of giant bats, hanging upside down, waiting to take off. Litter and glass crunched underfoot. Smiler looked at the state of the floor.

"Where are we supposed to sleep?" he asked.

It was obvious from the look on Jack's face, he hadn't thought this through. Palatine House had been regularly vandalised. We would have to clear the debris from the floor if we were going to make ourselves in any way comfortable.

"And I bet there are bugs," Smiler grumbled, "or *rats.*"

"Stop whining, will you?" Jack snapped. "There aren't any rats. We'll find som…"

He didn't finish the sentence. He'd been interrupted by a noise none of us would ever have expected.

"It can't be," Jack murmured.

But there it was again. Somebody was playing the piano. It was just a handful of notes, a short, plaintive phrase.

"What is it?" Smiler wondered out loud.

"One thing's for sure," I said. "It isn't Madness."

Jack was gazing up the staircase into the gloom. "It's coming from up there. I don't get it. Who'd be playing the piano at this time of night?"

"There's something else you're forgetting," I said, a slight shake in my voice. "Did either of you ever notice a piano?"

Jack and Smiler shook their heads slowly.

"OK," Jack said. "You win. We're getting out of here."

No sooner were the words out of his mouth, than the heavy oaken door slammed shut. Jack hurried over and twisted the door handle.

"It's jammed," he said.

Suddenly I wasn't the only one to have a shake in his voice.

"Here," I said. "Let me try."

I twisted and turned the door handle. It didn't budge. I tried pulling. I even gave it a kick. It wasn't jammed. It was locked, from the outside.

"Who's there?" I shouted. "This is some kind of stupid joke, right?"

My voice echoed shrilly through the house.

"Is that you, Andy?" Jack asked, grasping at straws. Nobody thought Andy was the kind of kid to come all this way to put the wind up his mates. "Look, you've put the wind up us. Just open the door, OK?"

There was no answer. I knew this wasn't Andy's doing. Deep inside, I knew it was no practical joke either. Jack and I were still struggling with the door when I felt Smiler tugging at my sleeve. I turned to see what he wanted. In that same split-second, my scalp froze. Palatine House was no longer the vandalised ruin we had entered. Gas lights illuminated the immense hallway. We weren't standing on broken glass and rubbish, but on plush, crimson carpets. The walls weren't spray-canned and blackened by damp but freshly wallpapered. Immaculately polished furniture lined complemented the décor. The smashed window panes had been replaced by perfect glazing.

"What's going on?" Jack said. "This can't be happening."

"Look here," Smiler said, holding up a newspaper.

"Where did you find *that?*" I demanded.

Smiler pointed to a mahogany table. Lying on the surface was a pair of black, leather gloves and a woollen scarf. An umbrella was propped in a stand next to the table.

"Read the date," Smiler said.

I took the paper from him. It was a copy of The Times, dated April 28th, 1882. I knew from the feel of the paper that this was no museum artefact. It was crisp and new. It hadn't even been opened.

"April 28th," I said. "That's tonight."

Then I noticed something else. Written across the top of the newspaper, in perfect copper-plate handwriting, was a name. Rathmore.

"Oh God," I said.

"What is it?" Smiler asked.

I held out the newspaper.

"Rathmore," I said. "You don't think those stories are true, do you?

Jack, usually so cocky, was dumb-struck. He was standing at the bottom of the stairs, his face pale and wan. Then he broke his silence.

"Lads," he whispered.

We followed the direction of his gaze. Coming down the stairs, barefoot and wearing a nightdress, was a young girl. She couldn't have been more than nine years old. She plodded down the stairs and stopped about a metre from where Jack was standing.

"Who are you?" she asked. "How did you get in here?"

Jack opened his mouth but the words didn't come out.

"I'm Paul," I answered. "This is Smiler...I mean, Liam. That's Jack."

"You're trespassing," the girl said. "Papa will be very angry if he finds out." She glanced behind her then continued in hush tones. "He has these fearful rages sometimes."

Smiler and I exchanged looks of utter horror. Andy's stories were true. Before the girl could say another word, there was a heavy tread on the landing above our heads.

"Emily," a man's voice shouted, "what are you doing out of bed?"

"That's him now," Emily said. "You've got to get out of here. Go, before he comes to find me."

We didn't need telling twice. Smiler led the race for the door. Then he cried out in despair.

"The door," he groaned, "it's still locked."

Emily ran to the door and rattled the handle.

"Oh dear," she said. "You're right. That means you're going to have to face him."

The heavy tread was coming down the stairs. Slowly, hardly daring to breathe, Smiler and I turned round. Rathmore was a tall, lean man, standing well over six feet tall. He was wearing black trousers, black boots and a white shirt with a starched collar. His eyes were unsettlingly pale and blue and seemed to stare right through us.

"What's this, Emily?" he demanded. "Have you presumed to invite your friends to my house without asking permission?" He glanced at the grandfather clock. "And at this unearthly hour?"

"They-they were not invited," Emily stammered. "Look at them, Papa. They are rough, village boys. They must have broken in."

"That isn't true!" Smiler protested. "The door was open."

Rathmore's blue eyes flashed like splinters of ice.

"That's impossible!" he thundered. "The front door is always locked at precisely nine o'clock. After that time, nobody enters, nobody leaves. That is the rule of the house."

His stare roved over us.

"I am a fair-minded man," he said. "I will not punish all three of you. Tell me which of you is the ring-leader. Give him up and I will spare the others."

Jack gasped out loud.

"Well, well, that must mean he is standing next to me," Rathmore said, his eyes narrowing.

"No, I didn't get them to do anything," Jack babbled. He gazed at us pleadingly. "Tell him."

Smiler and I shifted our feet uneasily. Terror had us by the tongue. We didn't speak.

"Oh, please lads," Jack sobbed. "Don't leave me here. We're all in this together."

He took a step forward but Rathmore restrained him. I finally found my voice.

"What are you going to do to him?" I asked.

"He will be chastised," Rathmore said. "The attic serves as a punishment room."

At the mention of the attic, Emily started to tremble.

"You can't desert me like this," Jack said, struggling to break free of Rathmore's grip. "Please."

Rathmore handed Emily a key. "Unlock the door."

Emily did as she was told.

"Well," Rathmore asked, "what is your decision?"

Neither Smiler and I said a word. Closing our ears to Jack's terrified screams, we turned to go. It is twenty years since that night and I can still hear him pleading not to be left alone. But we took no notice of his begging. We put ourselves first and stepped into the night. The moment we crossed the threshold, everything changed. Palatine House was a ruin once again. Instinctively, I gazed up at the attic...and shuddered. After that, we ran all the way home.

The police were called. They searched Palatine House, but in vain. They even discovered the way into the attic. It was hidden behind a false wall. They found a nursery. It didn't seem that sinister, they said. But there was a collection of canes and walking sticks in a stand. They seemed out of place in a nursery. One day, about a month after that terrible night, Jack's Mum turned up at the school gates. She started screaming at us, saying we had something to do with her son's death. We lowered our eyes and let her accuse us. In a way, she was right. We had betrayed Jack. We had abandoned him to his fate.

The years have flown by. Smiler and I are still friends. Sometimes we take our own children up to the House of Fun, though never after dark. Once in a while I fancy I see Jack up there, in the attic window. He seems to be pounding against the glass, pleading to be set free. But I know that's impossible. He will be there for all eternity, the prisoner of the nursery, the victim of his dark master. Then I turn my back on the House of Fun, just as I turned my back on Jack all those years ago.

SANCTUARY

BY ALAN GIBBONS

"**W**hen I stand here looking out at the sea," Dad said, "it feels like we're the only people in the whole world."

Little did any of us know how close to the truth that was. It was our last day on Mona, a small island off the North West coast of Scotland. Dad knew the owners, the McGaheys, from his hippie days back in the Seventies. They came up with the idea for a house swap sometime last year during one of their reunions. During the February half term, the McGaheys would spend a week at our house overlooking the Gormley statues on Crosby beach and we would occupy their croft, the only house on Mona. The McGaheys had named it Sanctuary, the place where they escaped from the stresses of the modern world. I thought the McGaheys had got the best deal. So did my older sister Jennie. The McGaheys would get to see the sights of Liverpool. That included going to the Snow Patrol gig at the Echo Arena.

And what did we get? Two weeks with no TV, no mobile phone reception and no computers. The McGaheys had chosen to cut themselves off from civilisation up there on Mona, in their Sanctuary. They powered their croft by wind turbine and solar panels. They baked their own bread and made their own clothes from the wool from the island's flock of sheep. Once a month they crossed over to the mainland to phone friends from the local hotel. Mum and Dad thought it was marvellous. They loved the idea of going green, if only for a fortnight. Jennie and I thought it was naff. In fact, it was naff-issimo. It only had one good thing going for it. It saved our lives.

The day Dad made his big speech about being the only people in the world was our last day at Mum and Dad's precious Sanctuary. We got up at half past eight, had a bowl of cereal and a round of toast then went for a walk to say goodbye to Mona. After that, we locked the croft up even though there wasn't another human being on the island. I made some crack about sheep with ASBOs but nobody laughed. Then it was the half mile walk along the coastal path to the only way of reaching the mainland, an ageing motorboat that chugged over to a place called North Coast Berths where the McGaheys would pick it up.

"You know," Dad said, "I feel like a new man." He

patted his belly. "I think I might have lost a couple of pounds with all that walking."

It was wishful thinking. Dad was at least a stone overweight and a couple of weeks walking along a shingle beach wasn't going to make that much difference to his waistline.

Jennie snorted. "Walking's all there was to do, and it's freezing all the time."

"Don't be ungrateful," Mum said. "It wasn't that bad. We got to see the wild seals, didn't we?"

"That was one day," Jennie grumbled. "It rained the rest of the time."

"Not *all* that time," Dad said.

"Nearly," Jennie insisted. "You'd think they'd have a mobile phone mast up here. I've been out of the loop for two weeks. Can you imagine how much lovely gossip I've missed?"

Dad ruffled her blond hair. Jennie pulled back and scowled. She hates being treated like a kid.

"What about you, Tom?" Dad asked.

"It was OK," I said, "but I can't wait to get home and see my mates. Plus the footy season will be starting a week on Saturday."

We reached the jetty and loaded the boat evenly. The conditions were good for the crossing, not like the day we came over. It had been really choppy and Jennie kept threatening to throw up. She's a real drama queen, my sister. As we chugged across to the mainland, Mum and Dad cast a glance back at Mona. Jennie and I gazed straight ahead, waiting for our lives to restart after a fortnight's exile from the real world. Soon we were in sight of land. Dad squinted through the morning mist.

"I wonder if somebody's going to come out and guide us in," he said.

"I don't see anyone," Mum said.

"No." Dad frowned. "Odd that, the place was heaving the day we left."

"Hardly *heaving*," Jennie remarked.

She was right. Port Hawick had a population of less than five thousand. There are livelier graveyards.

"True," Dad said, "but there isn't a boat moving. See for yourself."

"Your Dad's right," Mum said, suddenly thoughtful. "There isn't a soul on the quay either." She drummed her fingers on the hull. "I could understand if it was a Sunday. You'd think there would be somebody about."

I could tell the pair of them were getting twitchy. I wondered what all the fuss was about. The people at the quay were probably just skiving somewhere. Big deal. It happens all the time.

"It looks like we're going to have to moor the boat ourselves," Dad said. "Go on, Tom. You're the youngest. Jump off and pass me that rope."

I did as I was told.

"Now that one."

In a couple of minutes we had moored the McGahey's boat and unloaded the luggage.

"It really is very quiet," Mum said, letting her gaze rove over the quayside. "What time is it?"

Dad glanced at his watch. "Eleven o'clock."

"So where is everybody?" I asked.

Jennie tossed her head and gave a loud groan.

"I thought you said I'd get mobile reception when we got back here," she said.

"You should do," Mum said. She fished for her

own mobile. "I phoned your aunty Helen from here on the way over. I got through OK then. Let me try. I'm with a different network." She pressed the set to her ear then shook her head. "That's two of us who can't get a signal."

Dad and I both tried, and failed, to get a signal.

"It just gets worse," Jennie complained. "I was really looking forward to catching up with the girls."

"Well, you'll just have to be patient a little bit longer," Mum said. "In three hours or so we'll be in Glasgow. The phones are bound to start working on the drive down."

Jennie rolled her eyes and stamped off towards the car.

"Don't forget your suitcase, madam," Dad told her. "We're not lugging it for you."

Jennie snatched up the case and resumed her petulant walk to the car. She's so good at throwing a strop. Dad glanced at me and pulled a face. I laughed. We had just finished stowing the luggage when Mum planted her hands on her hips, looked to right and left and shook her head.

"Look," she said, "you'll probably think I'm paranoid, but surely we should have seen somebody by now. I mean, listen. Do you hear anything?"

She was right. There was no traffic noise. There were no police or ambulance sirens. There was no music from TVs or radios. The only sound was the keening of the seagulls and the lap of the waves against the dock.

"Maybe we should explore," Dad said.

"Oh, do we have to?" Jennie moaned. "We can see just as well from the car."

Mum and Dad hesitated.

"She's got a point," Dad said finally. "I *am* in work tomorrow morning. It's a good seven or eight hours drive home, and that's if there aren't any hold-ups on the Motorway, which would be a minor miracle."

"Where are we stopping for dinner?" I asked.

"If you can hang on a few hours," Dad said, "we can pull in at Westmoreland Services. You like it there. We've got those sandwiches to tide us over."

"Deal," I said, climbing in the back with Jennie.

She had her arms folded huffily across her chest. She hadn't forgiven me for laughing at her. We'd gone about three streets when Dad hit the brakes.

"Now what?" Jennie demanded.

"See for yourself," Dad replied.

The road ahead was blocked. Half a dozen cars were slewed across the carriageway. Two had their doors open. It was as if the drivers had just got out and abandoned their vehicles. Dad unclipped his seatbelt and went over to have a look. He came back a couple of minutes later.

"Abandoned," he said. "The keys are still in the ignition of that Ford over there."

"I don't like the look of this at all," Mum said. "Something's wrong."

Even Jennie was starting to look concerned. "I still can't get a signal." She looked around. "Where are all the people?"

Dad was standing outside, leaning his hands on the roof of the car.

"This just doesn't add up," he said. "We haven't seen a single person since we arrived back from Mona." He glanced at his watch then leaned through the open window. "The news will be on. Switch over from that CD to FM. See if there's anything on the news."

Mum twisted the tuning button. At first there was nothing but white noise. Then she got something.

"The emergency continues.....your regional refuge centres....Portsmouth, Norwich, Cardiff, Milton Keynes..."

"Refuge centres?" Jennie said. "What the hell does that mean?"

Mum shushed her. "Let me listen."

The radio announcer continued to read the list of towns and cities. "...Manchester, Liverpool, Sheffield, Newcastle, Belfast, Edinburgh, Glasgow."

The signal faded and Mum twiddled the tuning button. "Make your way to the nearest regional refuge centre. There will be food and medical assistance. It is vital you do not find yourselves outdoors after dark. Repeat, you must not find yourselves outdoors after dark."

The Big Ben chimes followed then nothing. Mum surfed the airwaves for several minutes then gave up.

"That's it," she said. "What's happening here? What emergency? Why do they need refuge centres?"

"Maybe it's that Bird Flu," I suggested.

"Don't be stupid," Jennie said. "It wouldn't spread this quick. We've only been away two weeks. You don't think..."

"What?"

Jennie shrugged. "Maybe they've dropped the bomb."

All three of us stared at her.

"Don't be..."

Mum bit her lip. She said just the one word. "No, that's too far fetched."

Dad looked around. "You're right. There would be bomb damage, radioactivity."

"We're a long way north," Mum said. "A remote place like this might escape the worst of it."

"No," Dad insisted. "I've seen films. All the buildings would be flattened. The sky would be full of ash. Besides, we'd have seen a flash, a mushroom cloud, something."

"Well, if it isn't the Bomb," Jennie asked, "then what *has* happened?"

Nobody had an answer. Dad reversed the car to manoeuvre out of the road-block formed by the abandoned cars then mounted the pavement. We were just able to squeeze round the obstruction. As we bumped off the pavement again, Jennie leaned forward in her seat and pointed.

"It just goes on and on," she said.

She was right. Though they didn't completely block the road this time, dozens abandoned cars littered the road out of town.

"What the hell is going on?" Mum asked.

Dad shrugged. "We're not going to find out sitting here. So what do we do?"

"What *can* we do?" Mum said, answering his question with another of her own. "We may as well press on."

So press on we did. We'd been driving for a few minutes when Dad hit the brakes.

"Now what?" Jennie demanded, then her face drained of blood. "Oh God!"

There was an estate car right in front of us. But

this vehicle wasn't empty like the others. The driver was lying half-in, half-out of his seat, his head and shoulders resting on the roadway. There was a woman in the passenger seat, probably his wife, hanging loosely forward. Only her seatbelt stopped her cracking her head on the dashboard. Both looked dead.

"Stay there," Dad said.

"No Rob," Mum gasped. "Don't get out of the car."

"Dad," Jennie said, "don't be stupid."

"I've got to see if either of them are alive," Dad told them.

"Rob…"

Mum's voice faded into the morning air as Dad released his seat belt and set off towards the car. On impulse, I followed suit and raced after him. I heard Mum call my name but I kept on going. By the time I reached Dad's side, he was standing very still, eyes closed, pinching the bridge of his nose.

"What is it?" I asked, sensing the impact the scene in the car had had. Then I saw. "Oh…"

My voice trailed away. The man's throat had been torn open. Dried blood caked his shirt and formed a reddish brown pool around his head. The woman too had died violently. The lower half of her face had been completely ripped away and her chest gaped open. I realised what I was looking at. Her heart had been removed. I heard footsteps. It was Mum and Jennie. Dad spun round and tried to prevent them approaching any nearer.

"Well, what….?"

Jennie's scream interrupted Mum's question.

"Who could have done this?" I cried.

Mum was helping the sobbing Jennie back to the car. She turned and snapped a command at Dad. "Get Tom away from there. Do it now!"

Dad started to guide me away when I happened to notice something. The road ahead had been obscured by a Mercedes van. I pulled away from him and peered round the side of the van.

"Dad," I said, "look."

He came over and followed the direction of my gaze then pressed a finger to his lips.

"Say nothing," he told me.

"But they're going to see soon enough," I protested.

"I know," Dad said, "but you can see the state Jennie's in. Humour me, will you son?"

I nodded then glanced once more at the carnage ahead. Within the next couple of hundred yards there were at least three more bodies. Seagulls were pecking at an elderly man's eye sockets. A young woman was lying on the tarmac, as if crucified. I'd seen enough and followed Dad back to the car. Mum was in the back seat with Jennie. Dad did the telepathic parent thing with his eyes and Mum took the hint. She pulled Jennie closer, pressing my sister's face against her shoulder. Dad turned the key in the ignition and accelerated past the dead couple. Changing up through the gear box, he slalomed through the canyon of vehicles. There were more bodies. Thankfully, Jennie let Mum shield her eyes from the horror. After a few minutes the jumble of abandoned cars thinned and Dad was able to cruise along at seventy, only slowing occasionally to go round a stationary vehicle. After a while, Jennie sat up.

"What do you think happened back there?" she asked. Expecting Mum and Dad to stonewall, she added. "Look, I'm not a little kid any more. Neither is Tom. Who killed those people?"

"I don't think those wounds were inflicted by human beings," Mum said.

"What then?"

"I don't know," Mum said. "Those gashes reminded me of a dog bite, but much, much worse."

"But it can't be animal attacks," Jennie cried, "not on this scale."

She jabbed a finger at a lay-by where the crumpled bodies of a whole family lay, their clothing soaked with blood.

"You're right," Dad admitted. "Something terrible has happened while we've been on Mona, something I can't explain. All we can do is press on and hope to find somebody who can help us."

Nobody said much after that. We must have been driving for at least two hours when we saw the signs for Glasgow. Dad indicated and pulled over to the side of the road.

"What are you doing?" Jennie asked.

"We've got a decision to make," Dad said, pulling into the kerb. "We all heard that radio broadcast. There's supposed to be some kind of refuge centre in Glasgow. Either we make for that or we press on towards Liverpool."

"I say we go home," Mum said. "Glasgow's a big city. We wouldn't know where to start looking. Besides..."

"What?"

"There are bound to be more abandoned cars blocking the roads. What if we got stuck? We might be vulnerable to whatever has killed all those people. At least we know the roads back home."

"That's my view too," Dad said. "Well, you two, do you have anything to add?"

"I say we go home," I announced.

Jennie nodded. "Me too."

We stopped off once for a toilet break and something to eat. We parked on a clear stretch of road and took it in turns to eat the sandwiches. Mum and I kept look out while Dad and Jennie ate then we swapped places. I'd never felt so jittery in my whole life. All the time we were there in the open, I could feel my flesh crawling.

"Just one thing," Jennie said uneasily. "It's OK posting look-outs, but what are we looking *for*?"

"I only wish I knew," Dad said, "anything that moves, I suppose."

Jennie was gnawing anxiously at her bottom lip. Dad slipped his arms round her shoulders.

"We'll be all right," he said.

"How do you know?" Jennie asked, shrugging him away.

Dad didn't answer. In the quiet that followed, Mum turned and stared through the rear window.

"What is it?" I asked.

Mum frowned for a moment, shushing me with a wave of the hand. "Listen."

The sound was unmistakeable. It was the clatter of rotor blades.

"Helicopter!"

Dad and Jennie had heard it too. Soon, all four of us were out of the car. There, sweeping in from the west was a two-seater chopper. We started to wave. Jennie thought quicker than the rest of us, peeling off her jacket and using it as a flag. We followed suit.

"Hey," Dad shouted. "Hey!"

But the chopper pilot didn't notice us, either that, or he chose to ignore us.

"Why didn't he stop?" Jennie cried bitterly. "You saw how low he was. He must have seen us." She sank to her knees. "Why didn't he stop?"

Mum lifted her to her feet and guided her to the car.

"You sit with Jennie in the back," Mum said. "I'll do the driving. You need a break."

Dad nodded. We drove for another half an hour in silence. Soon we were in the northern Lake District.

"Nearly home," Dad said.

But the strange sight of thousands of cars and hundreds of dead bodies left us subdued. Whatever catastrophe had struck, it must have hit Liverpool too. Suddenly, Mum cursed. I had hardly heard her swear before that day. That added to the shock value.

"What is it?" I asked.

"We're running low on petrol." She pointed at the Motorway Services sign. "We're coming up to Westmoreland. It looks like we're going to stop off there after all."

"Can't we try to make it all the way home?" Dad asked. "I think we're safer if we keep moving."

Mum shook her head. "No chance. We're running pretty much on empty." Then her tone changed. "Look!"

I saw why she was so excited. About half a mile in front of us, a black Volkswagen was leaving the Motorway and pulling into the Services. We weren't alone.

"Maybe we're going to find out what the Hell is going on," Dad said.

We coasted through the car park, peering into the restaurant. There was no sign of life.

"Keep on going, Marie," Dad said. "Don't stop till we get to the petrol station."

We stopped at the pump. It was late afternoon and the winter light was fading. The VW was parked by the pump in front of us. There was no sign of the driver.

"There," Jennie said.

She was right. The driver, a woman of about twenty five, was in the shop. She had just finished filling a carrier bag with sandwiches and sausage rolls and she was starting on the bottled water. The way she was stuffing it all in told us she was scared out of her wits.

"You go," Dad said, starting to fill the tank. "She's less likely to be spooked by another woman."

Mum nodded and crossed the forecourt to the door. When she opened the door, the younger woman started. I saw her stiffen with fright then relax. Though I couldn't hear what was being said, the conversation seemed friendly enough. Jennie set off to join Mum when a strange, primal shriek broke the silence.

"What was that?"

The animal howl echoed through the gathering dusk. Jennie and I exchanged nervous looks. A second bestial shriek answered the first, this time seeming to come from the Services car park. Yet another echoed from within the restaurant. Simultaneously, Mum and the young woman she had been talking to came sprinting towards us. The colour had drained from both their faces.

"Drive!" Mum yelled.

"What?"

"You heard," Mum bawled. "Drive!" Her eyes were wide with terror. As she scrambled into the driver's seat, she called to the other woman. "Don't lose sight of us, Karen."

Our new companion nodded and jumped into the VW. As we pulled away, the chorus of howls rose into the night.

"Wolves?" I said. "There are no wolves in the UK."

Mum floored the accelerator. I'd never seen her drive so fast. Karen roared after us.

"Look!" Jennie said, from the back seat.

I turned. The car park was filling with silhouetted figures.

"But it seemed empty a minute ago," Dad said.

"Well, it isn't now," I murmured.

The shadowy outlines were moving quickly, racing after us.

"Who are they?" I asked.

Mum's answer stunned us all.

"You were half right, Tom," she said.

"About what?"

"The wolves," Mum replied. "That's what the radio announcement meant when it warned about going out after dark. They're... werewolves."

"What?"

Shock crackled through the air. This was Mum

talking, Mum who was always so logical, who always searched for a common sense explanation for everything, and here she was taking about monsters!

"You can't be serious," Dad spluttered.

"I'm deadly serious," Mum snapped. "They killed Karen's family. She saw her parents and her brother torn to shreds right in front of her. That's what happened while we were on Mona. The country has been overrun by a plague of werewolves."

"But that's impossible," Jen said.

"Really?" Mum said. "So how do you explain *them.*"

Everywhere I looked, the shadowy figures were moving in the thickening murk. Karen's headlights had just floated into view behind us as we swept down the M6. I stared at the speedometer. Mum had just hit ninety and she was still accelerating.

"Do we have to go quite so fast?" Dad asked from the back seat.

"If you'd heard Karen's story in full," Mum replied, "you wouldn't ask. I didn't get to tell you half of it."

I listened to their exchange for a moment then yelled a warning. Dozens of the fast-moving creatures were racing straight at us. Mum didn't slow. Driving at the thinnest part of the attacking swarm, she ploughed through.

Our headlights caught the beasts, illuminating their bared fangs, their bristly faces, their wild, scarlet eyes. One of the werewolves bounced off the bonnet, another spun away as the left wing clipped it.

"What about Karen?" Mum yelled.

"She's made it through," Jennie answered.

We careered on down the mountain gradient, engine screaming. Twice, packs of werewolves burst from the night. Both times Mum weaved a way through. I saw her in a new light.

"Were you a joy rider in another life?" I demanded.

Mum stared grimly ahead. She wasn't in any mood to exchange banter. We were approaching Lancaster when Mum started to slow.

"Mum," Jennie asked, "what are you doing?"

I saw why Mum was easing off the gas. Up ahead, a pack of werewolves were besieging a mini-bus. The passengers were trying to fight them off with anything they had to hand. Mum pounded the horn. Behind us, Karen did the same, then accelerated alongside. Together, the two cars hurtled into the creatures. Mum spun the car and drove back at the werewolves, crushing one against a lorry and running over two more. Karen simply reversed back over the ones she had hit. Either way, it seemed effective. Four of the mini bus's passengers piled into the VW. One sprinted over and clambered in next to Jennie. No time was wasted on introductions. With the door still swinging open, we roared away. The newcomer succeeded in slamming the door and gasped a thank you.

"I thought we were finished," he said. "I'm Greg, by the way."

Dad did the introductions then demanded to know what was happening.

"Where the Hell have you been?" Greg asked.

Dad explained.

"You've got to be the luckiest people alive," Greg told us. "It started five days ago…or was it six?

I'm losing count. I've hardly slept since the emergency began."

He described that first day, the incoherent, unbelievable news bulletins, the growing sense of panic.

"To begin with, everybody thought it was a spoof, like that radio programme in nineteen thirties America, when they broadcast War of the Worlds as if it was really happening. It was all too unbelievable."

"So that was Monday?" Dad asked.

"Yes, Monday," Greg confirmed, "the night of the full moon. Nobody knows what happened. But in every street there was at least one person who carried the infection. They transformed and started to infect other people."

"Infect?" Jennie asked. "What do you mean?"

"The dead are the lucky ones," Greg explained. "But if you get a flesh wound, it festers. Within twenty four hours, you have become a werewolf yourself. That's how it spread so fast. The police and the Army were just overwhelmed."

"But how did it begin?" Mum asked.

Greg shook his head. "Nobody knows. One thing's for certain, there are more of them than there are of us. By Wednesday, society was on the verge of collapse. By yesterday evening, the survivors had clustered into twenty or so refuge centres, fighting for their lives. We were heading to the one in Preston when we were attacked. You saved our lives."

Mum punched the car radio. "I just wish somebody was broadcasting. I don't want to drive into an ambush."

Greg pulled out a mobile. "I've got this."

"Forget it," Jennie said, "mobiles don't work any more."

"You should have kept trying," Greg said. "They do here. The Army have repaired a couple of the masts. It's poor but for the last 24 hours there has been some local coverage."

He punched in a number. A few seconds later the hope drained from his face.

"Preston must have fallen," he said. "Let's hope Liverpool is still holding out." He punched in a second number. "Hello. Thank God. This is Greg Scraggs on the M6. There are about ten of us. Can you come out and get us."

We could hear the crackle of a man's voice at the other end of the line. I saw Greg's expression. The answer was no. "OK, if we make it to Liverpool under our own steam, where do we go? The Albert Dock? I've heard of it but I've never been."

He glanced at Dad and Dad nodded.

"Yes," Greg said. "There's somebody here who knows the city. We can find our way there." He listened for a moment then switched off the mobile. "He says there are about five thousand survivors at the Albert Dock. The Army are constructing a ring of steel. We've got three hours to reach them. After that, we don't get in. There will be a complete lock-down. They're calling it Sanctuary."

Jennie rolled her eyes. "Not again."

"What?"

"Don't worry about it, Greg," I said. "It's a private joke."

Forty five minutes later we branched off onto the M58.

"Not long now," Dad said in a clumsy attempt to reassure us.

But we all knew that the city would be far more dangerous than the Motorway. The roads would be narrower and the werewolves more numerous. We were about to enter the eye of the storm. About a mile from Switch Island, the northern gateway to the city, Karen flashed us. Mum slowed and Karen pulled alongside. Winding down her window, she said her piece.

"Your driving's amazing," she said.

Mum nodded grimly. "I had a bit of a wild youth."

This was news to me and Jennie. We stared at Dad. He pulled a face. If he knew what she was talking about, he wasn't saying.

"How far is it to this refuge centre?" Karen asked.

"Seven or eight miles," Mum answered.

"And is it all through city streets?"

"Yes," Mum confirmed, "most of it."

One of Karen's passengers flopped back in his seat. "We aren't going to make it."

"Shut up!" Karen snapped. "That's the last thing I want to hear right now." She thought for a moment. "We need weapons. I don't see us getting through without them. The werewolves are capable of building a barricade. That's how they killed my family."

There was a long silence then I remembered something.

"Uncle Mark knows about guns," I said.

Mark was Dad's brother.

"He does," Dad said, "but God knows if he's still alive."

"That's not what I'm getting at," I said. "Where does he do his shooting?"

"He doesn't any more," Dad said. "He used to be in the Territorial Army." His eyes widened. "Of course, they'll have guns and ammunition at the TA Centre."

"Are you sure?" Mum asked.

"No," Dad admitted, "I'm not but do you have a better idea?"

That's how we settled on the idea of breaking into the TA Centre...and how we came face to face with the werewolves.

"Follow me in," Mum said.

We drove fast. There were a couple of werewolf attacks but we kept on going. It took us twenty minutes to reach the TA Centre.

"It looks quiet," Jennie said, gazing across the carriageway at the squat, yellowish building.

"So did the road when the werewolves ambushed us," Greg said.

"How do we do this?" Karen wondered out loud.

Mum took the lead. "We'll stay in the cars. We might need to get out of here quickly. Greg, you and your friends go inside to get the guns."

Greg shook his head. "You want me to get out of the car, you mean? There's no way. My nerves are shot."

Mum was furious. "Do you want to live, or not?"

Dad intervened. "There's no point bullying him. You've got to be one hundred per cent committed to carry off something like this. I'll do it."

"You?" I gasped.

"Have you got a better idea?" Dad demanded. I

don't think he liked the surprise in my voice. Well, he'd never exactly been Action Man.

"Rob…"

"Please love,"

Mum stared at him for a moment, then she nodded. "But the kids stay with me."

I tried to protest but Dad cut me off. "Your Mum's right."

With that, he got out and produced a wheel brace from the boot. One of the men from the other car did likewise. Another man and one of the women had to make do with the car jacks from each boot. They looked faintly ridiculous, but they were the only weapons available. Without a backward look, the quartet set off. For long minutes, we sat on the edge of our seats, staring at the darkened building. Suddenly, there were a couple of loud reports. Simultaneously, lurid flashes lit the windows. Mum glanced at Karen.

"Start your engine," she said.

A moment later, two people emerged from the building. They were armed.

"Is one of them Dad?" Jennie asked.

Mum shook her head.

"There he is!" I cried.

It wasn't good news. The two men were racing ahead. The woman was catching hard on their heels. But Dad, overweight by over a stone and older than the others, was toiling. At least a dozen werewolves were on the brink of outflanking him.

"Dad!" Jennie screamed.

Dad skidded to a halt and fired twice. Two of the monsters slumped to the ground. Mum drove at the werewolves, bumping over the body of one.

"Reverse!" Greg screamed. "We'll be trapped."

"That's my husband," Mum shrieked at him, "the father of my children."

She slammed into another of the creatures. Already, more of them were pouring from the building, surrounding us. A volley of shots rang out from Karen's car. The head of the nearest werewolf exploded. It didn't deter the rest of the creatures. They were flinging themselves at the car. One of the windows was cracked already.

"If we stay," Greg howled, "they're going to kill us all."

"Go!" Dad yelled, firing point black into the chest of one of the predators. "You can't get to me."

"I won't leave you!" Mum cried.

Then Dad did the only thing he could to force her to go without him. Shaking his head, he plunged back into the TA Centre, pursued by a host of snarling werewolves.

"Rob!"

"You've got to go," Greg yelled. "What's the point of us all dying? Face it, your husband's gone."

Mum spun round, her face full of hatred. But Greg played the winning card.

"Listen to me," he said, his face hard. "Do you want to lose your children too?"

Mum glared at him for a moment then, face awash with tears, she spun the car and drove off. We led the way into the city. The following vehicle covered us with rifle fire. I'm not sure how accurate the novice shooters were but they managed to nail enough of the werewolves to clear a path. Finally, we saw the Albert Dock. Soldiers ran to open the hastily constructed gate that led into the military compound. Mum roared inside and slewed the car across the cobbled street. Karen followed. We gathered together, exhausted but alive. That's when Mum did it. She strode right up to Greg and slapped him across the face.

"You're the one who should have died inside that building," she screamed. "You're not worth the dirt on my Rob's shoes."

Greg hung his head. I saw the tears spilling down his cheeks. We spent the next hour sitting on a kerb stone, listening to the rattle of machine guns as the soldiers defended the refuge centre from wave after wave of the werewolves. Finally, dawn lit the sky.

Jennie shook her head.

"Look at that," she said. "Greg was right about the mast. I've got a signal."

Mum and I switched our phones on and stared at them. It seemed such a long time since we had first discovered we couldn't make any calls. Mum was just slipping the phone into her jacket pocket when it buzzed. She stared in disbelief.

"I've got a text!"

"Let me see," I cried.

Jennie crowded in too. There was one word on the screen: *Sanctuary*.

"It can't be," Mum said.

At that moment the sun rose and thunderous applause echoed across the Dock. Mum led the way as we raced to the main gates. Reassured by the bright sunlight, the guards opened up. A band of survivors were jogging towards us. Some were bloodstained. The first half dozen fell into the arms of the soldiers who had run out to meet them. But it was the last man in the group we were waiting for, the oldest, slowest and least fit of the group. It was Dad.

"This time," he panted as he threw his arms round us, "I think I really have lost a few pounds."

Nobody was arguing.

MERCY

BY ALAN GIBBONS

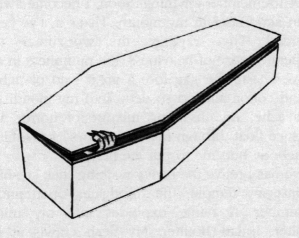

I wake to darkness. I feel myself frown, my forehead rumpling in puzzlement, and some unease. My surroundings are unfamiliar. It is not just that it is dark. There is a complete absence of light. There is no ray of moonlight, no glow of a street lamp, no flicker of a guttering candle. As my eyes become accustomed to the darkness, I gradually begin to make out a textured surface above me. I follow the barely visible swirls. It's a wooden surface. Yes, that's what it is. It's some kind of lid. So I am in a box. That begs more question than it answers. I am in a box. But what am I doing here? Who put me here?

My mind races. At first there is no answer to my

questions. There is a shadow of the truth. It lurks just out of sight, a tantalising, teasing, presence. It is like that moment when you recognize somebody in the street but can't quite recall their name. Why don't I remember anything? Soon, I become aware of an acrid taste in my mouth. That's it, I've been drugged. That explains the wooziness, the desperate sense of heaviness, the numbness in my limbs. I taste the gag too, a great wad of tightly bound cotton shoved so deep into my mouth my jaws ache. An unsettling mixture of horror and injustice float through the back alleys of my mind. Somebody hurt me to put me here.

Even as I relive the heavy walking stick crashing against my temple, the floodgates open and I remember. A name explodes into my mind. Boulter. Isaiah Boulter. My flesh crawls at his name. Isaiah Boulter, the undertaker, my employer. The details of my story bob to the surface like sunken boats recovered from the bottom of the Thames. I am Henry Scraggs. I was born on August 14th, 1842. My senses swim for a moment. I become aware of the dried blood on my forehead and in my hair. I imagine the events that must have followed the moment he felled me with that stick of his. I'm a scrawny cove, short and ill fed. It won't have cost Boulter much effort to carry or drag my bony little body into the funeral parlour. He'll have dumped me into this coffin like a side of meat and screwed it down tight. The first chance he gets, he'll bury me alive, the way he did the others.

That's what it's about, see. He could have killed

me any time he wanted. But that ain't his game. Boulter's a monster. He drugs his victims and buries them alive. The only reason he hit me with the stick is because I struggled free of him before that potion of his could work. I started howling and yelling for help. I was making such a racket I'd have had the Bobbies down on him so he gave me a hefty crack across the skull. That's how I ended up here, gagged and bound in one of his caskets.

My arms are tingling. My wrists are sore where a rope has chafed the skin. He's got me trussed up like a Christmas turkey, the foul and evil rogue. I start to cry, cold tears spilling down my cheeks. Why didn't I take more notice of the warnings Emily gave me? Was it because her story was just too fantastical to believe?

I entered my master's house eight long months ago. From the very first, I was terrified of the monster. He plucked me from the workhouse. I never knew my old Dad. He was killed in an accident down St Katherine's Dock when I was a babe in arms. My mother passed away last winter of a fever. There was nobody else to take me in so I passed into slavery. Believe me, that's no exaggeration. Boulter allowed us children only six hours sleep and precious little food. We toiled from dawn to dusk and, should we ever complain about our lot, he would beat us severely.

It was some months before I had an inkling what Boulter was up to. The children he used to labour for him came and went. Once in a while, one of us would be brave enough to ask where such and such had gone, but Boulter would only fly into a rage and thrash whoever had dared speak up. We soon stopped asking. But we knew something was wrong. We knew they hadn't gone on to other masters. Boulter had done for them somehow.

It was Emily who discovered the truth. She came running in to me just a few nights ago, her face white with terror. She'd surprised old Boulter, carrying poor little Oliver Strensham into the funeral parlour. Emily screamed at Boulter, demanding to know what he was doing. Boulter said Oliver had fallen and broken his neck but Emily knew it wasn't true. She could see Ollie was warm and still breathing. That must have been when Boulter decided to get rid of her too. This morning I saw two coffins in the parlour. One was for Emily. The other was for me. Boulter wasn't taking any chances. Knowing Emily had told me what his game was, he had to get shut of both of us. Like a fool, I did nothing. I was too scared. Now I'm lying here, bound and gagged, waiting for Boulter to take me away and put me six feet under.

A terrible weariness comes over me. Why fight? There's no way I can break out of these bonds. I may as well just give in. What happens to you when there ain't no air to breathe? Does it hurt, I wonder, or do you just go to sleep? That might be for the best. It would be an end to my troubles if I just passed away in my sleep. Maybe there's a Heaven up there above the clouds. Maybe my parents are there, waiting to welcome me. Maybe...

But I don't believe it. What's wrong with you,

Henry Scraggs? Are you soft in the head or something, you good for nothing rascal? Are you just going to lie there and let some good-for-nothing beast like Boulter do for you? It just ain't right. Why should he get away with it? That ain't all. Emily might still be breathing. What kind of lousy coward lies down and dies when his only friend in this bleak, cold world is in another casket in this very same room, pleading to be set free? I won't let you suffer, Emily. I'm going to set you free, you see if I don't.

In that moment, I start to struggle. I wriggle and twist and writhe in my bonds until I am exhausted. Then, as I lie here panting, I start to think more clearly. It ain't no use just threshing about like a fish on a river bank. There's got to be a purpose to what I'm doing. I breathe deeply, trying to settle myself. Right, Henry my lad, think. Picture yourself in this here parlour. What does Boulter do with his coffins? He puts them up on these trestle tables. Come to think of it, they ain't that stable. Many's the time I've had to set them out. Shake them too much and they come crashing to the floor. That's it. If I can rock from side to side, I might just succeed in toppling the table over.

It's worth a try. I start rocking, over to the left, over to the right. Did you hear that, Henry, you just made a table leg scrape on the stone floor. You little gem, you! Oh, we ain't done yet, Emily, not by a long chalk. I keep up the rocking and suddenly I feel dizzy. That must be the table tilting. I'm nearly there. Once more ought to do it….and it does! The whole kit and caboodle comes crashing down. The side of the casket splits. Well, look at that! You thought you were saving money, didn't you Boulter, holding back the better quality coffins for your paying customers? That was your first mistake.

I wriggle and squirm onto my side with my back to the split and force my bound hands up to the opening. My fingers are tingling but there's enough strength left in them to start tugging at the gap. There's a satisfying splintering sound. The casket's coming apart. I work on it. Seconds tick by. Minutes. I keep working. My fingernails are screaming with pain but I won't stop. Boulter didn't come running when the coffin tumbled to the floor but he could be back any time. I can't rest. I daren't. Emily could be listening this very moment, hoping I'm going to come to the rescue. I won't let you down, Emily. I swear, I'm going to get you out.

There's another loud crack and the whole side of the flimsy casket gives way. I slide my body backwards, scuffling against the stone floor with my bare feet. Oh, you beauty! The light hurts my eyes. Bright sunlight. It was going dark when Boulter laid about me with his stick. I've been in that box all night. If it's morning, he'll be buying materials. If it's afternoon, he'll be feeding the horse, getting ready to transport the coffins down to St Mary's yard. My gaze roves round the parlour. There's Emily's coffin. I just pray she's still alive. She should be. That's Boulter's savage crusade, to bury them alive. Then my eyes alight on the saw in the corner, the one we use to cut the wood to size.

There's no time to waste. Even now, Boulter could be on the way down the steps. The parlour is in his cellar, most likely because nobody can hear his victim's cries down here.

I rub my bonds up and down. Twice I catch my skin on the teeth of the saw and feel the blood run. I bite my lip so I don't cry out. Then, in one glorious moment of release, I'm free.

Pulling the gag from my mouth and untying the knots to free my legs, I stagger to my feet. Simultaneously, I hear the door slam. It's Boulter. I stumble over to the other coffin.

"Emily," I whisper, "are you in there? Do you hear me?"

Nothing.

"Em…"

Before I can finish the word, there is a thump against the wall of the coffin. Though I can't make out what she's saying because of the gag in her mouth, I know it's her.

"Lie still," I hiss. "Don't say a word."

Reassuring myself that Emily is going to lie still, I search for a weapon. The saw wouldn't be much use. But that's all there is. Boulter doesn't keep his tools in here. He takes great care to lock them away every night. He doesn't want one of his slaves picking up a hammer and smashing the master's head in. There are the smashed bits of coffin but it's such a shoddy, flimsy affair it would probably just break on Boulter's head without doing one iota of damage.

His boots scrape on the stairs. My heart misses a beat. No, not yet. I need more time. Oh think,

Henry, you've come this far. You can't have it all torn away from you now. Boulter curses. He's forgotten something. I listen as the hobnails scrape. He's turning round. He's climbing back upstairs. There, you've got a few moments to think, my old son. I can't risk trying to free Emily. The noise would bring the scoundrel running. I creep over to the door. Instinctively, I turn the door knob. It's open. Of course, why would he lock it? He had the two of us nailed down in our caskets. He had nothing to fear, did he? I creep up the stairs. All I have to do is hide behind the door when he opens it and give the blighter one almighty shove. With any luck, he'll break his rotten neck.

A minute passes, maybe two, then there he is. I hear the heavy tread. I smell the sweat sour on his overfed body. Come on, Boulter you pig. It's just you and me now. One of us is going to die. Frankly, I've been given a second chance. I was dead and now I'm walking. At least I'll go down fighting. But if there's the faintest chance I can bring you down, I will.

The door creaks open. His shadow appears on the steps. I hold my breath. Through the door he comes. I see his velveteen jacket. He grunts with surprise as the door bounces back. He has just started to peer round to see what's in the way when his eyes widen.

"What in God's name...?"

I throw myself against him with all my might but it doesn't go to plan. Instead of plunging down the stairs, he makes a grab for me and we fall together. I land on top of him. The heavy tumble knocks the breath out of him and I try to scramble away. To my horror, his fat fingers close round my ankle. He's got a grip like a vice. I yelp with pain.

"I'm going to enjoy making you suffer," Boulter snarls.

He brings his huge fist down on my shoulder. I scream in agony. He brings the fist down again. This time I roll back just at the right time and he punches the floor. It's his turn to shriek with pain. I kick him in the teeth and claw at the stone floor, trying to get away. His broken fingernails scrape against my bare feet. I kick for all I'm worth but he's just too strong. He's dragging me towards him. I see the smirk cross his blunt, cruel features. He knows he's won. He's going to savour the moment.

"I'm sorry, Emily," I sob, "so sorry."

Boulter chuckles and glances at the coffin...just in time to see it come crashing down on top of him. The corner crunches into his eye socket and he reels backwards. Oh Emily, you beauty. You took a leaf out of my book. Boulter makes the same noise the pigs do when the butcher cuts their throats down Whitechapel. Emily is staring at me, her eyes bulging. She's trying to tell me something. I yank out the gag.

"Finish him, Henry," she cries. "Either you finish him or he'll finish us."

I know what to do. The monster is keening with pain. I run up the steps and grab the claw hammer he keeps in the front room. I've never dared go near it until now. I run back down the steps and there he is, still rolling round clutching his eye.

"Do it!" Emily pleads.

I stare down at him, my hand trembling as I grip the hammer.

Hours later, we are sitting down by the Thames, watching the full moon bob in the water. Behind us, Boulter's broken down cart horse, Plodder is snorting and pawing the ground. We've just returned from burying Boulter in one of the graves he dug for us. Once we've got our breath, we're going to get Plodder out of the shafts and climb on his back. Emily's got a distant aunt who lives out Kent way. Suspicious about Boulter, she came looking for Emily once but Boulter locked Emily away and said she had run off. Nobody will come after us. There's hardly a soul who knows we even exist.

Oh, and if you're wondering about Boulter, we had the same thought about him, that it would be poetic justice to bury him alive. We considered it…and rejected the idea. I put the rogue out of his misery. It took one blow. I showed him something he never showed another soul.

Mercy.

MOUSETRAP

BY ALAN GIBBONS

1

Click! Chris was snatched out of sleep by that one tiny sound. His eyelids snapped wide open and he looked round the darkened room. He didn't see anything. As sounds go it wasn't the loudest. Nor was it the most unusual and it shouldn't have been in any way threatening. It wasn't the noise itself, you see. It was the *timing* that was wrong. There, on the tower, an amber light was flickering. Odd, Chris thought. A computer doesn't just come on in the middle of the night, not all by itself anyway. Machines are machines. They do what you tell them. But this machine was doing as it liked. Chris rubbed his eyes and sat up in bed. He listened to the computer as it went through its start-up sequence.

Click. Electricity fizzed through the machine.

Whirr. The motor kicked in and the cooling fan started.

Bleep. The disc drive hummed faintly and a small light, like a single green eye, winked in the darkness of the room.

"Now that can't be right," Chris said out loud.

It wasn't right. The computer continued to boot up, all by itself, and nothing it did was quite right. It's not that it did anything wildly out of the ordinary. But it was doing it by itself, that's the point. The whole thing was somehow off-kilter. Nobody had come in the room. Nobody had touched the mouse or the keyboard. Yet still it continued to start up. The printer carriage chattered along the track. The screen cleared and started to glow. There, just as he had thought. Quite by itself the computer had come on.

Chris didn't do anything. What was there to do? His mind sprinted through the various possibilities. Maybe there was a short circuit. Maybe the machine had a remote control and Dad was playing stupid games. Chris's mind was working overtime. Did computers have remote controls?

Don't be stupid, he told himself. Not on a model this old they don't. He was snatching at straws. Remote control, my foot! The PC was second hand; yes, second hand and maybe five years old. Dad had picked it up cheap from a car boot sale. Chris had been delighted when Dad brought it home.

It had everything: printer, scanner, loads of games to go with it. He wasn't delighted now. The PC was on. A lurid, pale green glow spilled from the screen and lit the room. It was as if it had been searching Chris out, making a connection. Well, the connection was made. Chris recognized the computer and the computer recognized Chris. Each was thinking the same thing:

You're alive!

2

"Come again?"

Dad looked up from his breakfast and fixed Chris with a doubtful stare.

"The computer," Chris repeated, "it came on by itself."

"When?"

"In the middle of the night. It woke me up."

"Sure," said Dad, "and your socks have just walked down here by themselves."

He gnawed at a rasher of bacon.

"Oh no, my mistake," he said, "you were in them at the time, weren't you?"

"Da-ad," Chris moaned, "I'm not joking. It started up all by itself about two o'clock."

"What you mean," Mum said, "is you were up playing on it until the small hours."

"Yes," Dad said. "Then your mind started playing tricks."

"No way," Chris protested. "Why do you always think it's down to me when something weird happens?"

It was a daft question. When was the last time anything this weird had happened?

"I had an early night," Chris went on, "honest. I was asleep the moment my head touched the pillow. It's a big match today."

The conversation slid away to the match. It was Sunday morning and Chris's team was in with a shout at the Under-fourteen title. No way was he going to mess that up. There might even be a scout watching.

"Anyway," Dad said. "Get your footy kit, son. We'd better make a move."

Chris nodded and jogged upstairs. He folded his kit and shoved it in his sports bag. He was just checking the studs on his boots when he heard a familiar sound.

Click!

Chris turned and stared at the computer monitor. Technical words and meaningless numbers chattered across the black screen. There were slashes, obliques, colons. Instinctively, Chris glanced round.

"Dad?" he said.

He still hadn't quite removed the idea from his mind. Was it at all possible that this was one of the old man's dumb practical jokes?

"What?"

That was Dad's voice drifting up from downstairs. Practical joke? No, that didn't explain it.

"Nothing."

Chris went over to the PC. He moved the mouse round the pad and selected *Shut down*.

Nothing happened.

Unease started to prickle down Chris's spine. He stared at the mouse and it was as if it really was a living creature, twitching its tail and watching him with mischief in its eyes. But it didn't have eyes, did it? It was a piece of machinery, that's all.

"Are you ready?" Dad called.

"Just a minute," Chris replied. "I think the PC has crashed."

"Oh, you've never been playing on it again," Dad moaned. "We're in a hurry. We've only got five minutes."

Chris clicked *Shut down* again. The computer didn't shut down, quite the opposite. With a loud chatter, almost a cackle, the printer juddered to life. A sheet of A4 paper slid out like a white tongue. Chris read it and his face drained of blood. It read:

"Have a good game."

3

Chris did not have a good game. He had a lousy game. He fluffed a shot, missed most of his tackles and blazed the best chance of the match over the bar. He was just lifting his leg to strike the ball when he saw something scurry across the pitch in front of him- a mouse. That's when he really did think he was going mad. All in all he had a real stinker of a game. Good job he was the only player in the team to perform below his best. Otherwise, they wouldn't have been crowned champions. To top it all, there *was* a scout, but Chris wasn't going to impress, not on that performance.

"Is there something on your mind, son?" Dad asked on the way home.

"Why do you ask?"

"Because," Dad said. 'In the most important game

of the season you played your worst football. That's with a scout watching, too. What gives?"

Chris shrugged. There didn't seem much point repeating the computer story. Dad hadn't believed him the first time round. Why would it be any different this time?

"Come on, son, let me in on it."

"I told you, Dad, there's nothing the matter."

"OK, suit yourself," said Dad.

He sounded disappointed. They didn't speak for the rest of the journey. Five minutes later Dad hung a left and pulled up in front of the house.

"But if you do want to talk," Dad said as they got out, "you know where I am."

Chris followed Dad into the house. He didn't want to talk.

For the next hour he found all sorts of excuses for not going up to his room. He stayed longer than usual at the dinner table. He watched a TV programme, and early Sunday afternoon the TV is awful. He even did some of his homework on the kitchen table. But he couldn't put it off forever. He had some IT to do and that meant using the computer.

With a sigh he plodded upstairs. He thought he heard a squeak as he came to the door but he shook the idea out of his head. He had a good idea what he was going to see when he walked in the room, and he was right. The computer was already on, waiting for him. It was playing a short cartoon clip. It showed a footballer. The player took the ball down on his chest, leaned back and...blazed it over the bar.

"Just the way I did," Chris said out loud.

That was the cue for the computer to answer. The computer chattered. A sheet of paper slid from the printer and dropped onto the tray. The machine was pulling tongues at him again.

"Two left feet," it read.

4

Chris got home from school the following afternoon about half past four. He was clutching the computer game his best mate Sean had given him.

"You're not playing that until you've done your homework and had your tea," Mum said.

Who's arguing, Chris thought.

He'd only accepted the stupid game because Sean would have been put out if he hadn't. All day at school he'd been seeing sheets of crisp white paper sliding out of the printer. He had hardly been able to think of anything else.

"I'll do my homework now," said Chris. "What time's tea?"

Mum stared at him. What was this, Chris *volunteering* to do his homework! He even carried on with it after tea. He was still at it when Dad came home.

"What's this?" Dad said. "Do I see Chris doing his homework on time? I could have sworn I saw a flying pig on the way home."

"It isn't that unusual," Chris grumbled. "I always get it done eventually."

"I'm only having a bit of fun," Dad said. "You don't have to be so touchy."

But Chris was touchy, touchy like the blue paper on a firework. The PC was making him touchy.

"You can play that game now, you know," Mum said.

"That's all right," said Chris. "I don't feel like it just now."

An image of the computer filled his mind. He could see the wink of its green light. He could hear the rattle of the carriage and the wheeze of the fan. He even thought he could hear the scamper of the mouse.

"It's not like you to sit down here when you've got a new game," Dad said.

Chris stood up, knocking his chair back.

"OK, OK," he snapped. He knew he was going way over the top.

"I'll play the stupid game. Happy now?"

Well, that was clever; Chris thought the moment he reached the top of the stairs. He could just imagine Mum and Dad exchanging confused glances. Still, it was too late to do anything about it now. Taking a deep breath, he pushed open the door. He looked at the PC and it looked straight back at him.

"You don't scare me, you know," Chris said. "You're a machine, that's all."

But the game was still in his hand when the computer started up.

By itself.

5

"Why can't I keep my big mouth shut?" Chris said out loud.

The noises coming from the PC seemed to speed up. Static electricity fizzed and crackled from the screen, buzzing cobwebs of energy. It was as though it was excited. It couldn't wait to answer him back. The answer came quickly enough. One by one keys were depressed as if by invisible fingers. Slowly a message formed on the screen:

You, keep your mouth shut? Fat chance!

Then, a split-second later came a second communication:

That's your problem.

In spite of himself, Chris took a step back.

"No," he said, "I'm not falling for it. You're not going to freak me out."

The invisible fingers tapped out a new message:

Sure about that?

It was the killer question. Of course he wasn't sure. He wasn't sure of anything any more, only that there was something seriously strange about the computer. Then it got stranger. The invisible fingers flickered over the keyboard. Chris looked at the screen.

Want to play?

Chris glanced away from the screen.

'What do you think?' he said.

The keyboard chattered. Chris looked back at the screen.

Want to play? Want to play? Want to play? Want to play? Want to play?

The answer was no, of course, but Chris couldn't force the word out. The keyboard chattered again.

Oh, come on. You're not chicken, are you? Let's play.

Chris stared at the message.

"Right," he said. "That does it."

He marched across the room and yanked the plug from the socket.

"Now," he said with some satisfaction, "stop arguing."

The computer fizzed and died. Chris looked at the blank screen and smiled. That shut you up, didn't it? Spinning round on his heel, he was about to march in triumph from the room when he heard a familiar sequence of sounds:

Click, whirr, beep.

"What the..!"

He turned and stared. The screen glowed. There was a hint of menace about it.

"This is impossible."

The keyboard clattered.

Nothing's impossible.

But if anything was impossible, this was. A computer can't work without power, Chris thought. It can't!

But the screen glowed. The disc drive hummed. Then the keys flattened and words appeared on the screen:

I *am* the power.

"What are you?" Chris stammered.

Then a thought occurred to him.

"Who are you?"

In reply the scanner flashed and a sheet started to shudder from the printer. Chris watched as an image formed. Finally the printer clicked and the sheet dropped into the tray. Chris had his answer.

He took the sheet and looked at it in horror. Dark

eyes stared back from a gaunt, almost fleshless face. Chris was still taking in what had happened when the invisible fingers tapped out another message.

Happy now?

Chris looked on while the computer shut itself down.

He was anything but.

6

Halfway through English Mr Harris came up behind Chris.

"What's more interesting than *Midsummer Night's Dream?*" he asked.

Chris turned round.

"Do you really want me to answer that?" he asked.

Mr Harris grinned. He was OK. He was one of those teachers who went with the flow. He would have a joke with you.

"So what are you reading?" Mr Harris asked.

"I'm not reading," Chris said. "I'm looking."

"Can I see?" said Mr Harris.

Chris hesitated then handed him the picture he'd got from the scanner. Mr Harris' expression changed. The blood fell from his face. The tone of his voice changed too.

"Come and see me at the end of the lesson," he said.

His voice had gone cold.

"Why?" Chris asked. "Have I done something wrong?"

"Just see me at the end of the lesson," Mr Harris repeated.

"But…."

"We'll talk at the end of the lesson, Chris."

Chris was aware of the rest of the class looking at him. His face burned. Finally the bell rang. When the room had emptied he walked to the front.

"Sir?" said Chris.

"This photograph," said Mr Harris. "Where did you get it?"

"It was on my computer."

"You mean you found it on the Internet?"

There didn't seem much point trying to explain about computers that go bump in the night, so Chris said:

"Yes."

"Do you know who this is?" Mr Harris asked.

Chris shook his head. "It was just a mug shot. I thought it looked…sinister."

"Oh, he was sinister all right."

"Do you know who he is?" Chris asked, even though it was obvious from his teacher's face that he did.

Mr Harris nodded. "I taught him."

"Who is he?"

"John McLeish."

Chris frowned. The name seemed familiar somehow.

"I see you recognize the name," said Mr Harris.

Chris nodded. "Yes, I'm sure I've heard of him. I just can't remember when."

"It happened five years ago," said Mr Harris. "McLeish had left school by this time. He was doing a home visit as part of his job. He got into an argument with the customer. He killed the poor man. It doesn't surprise me. Even as a kid he was, well, difficult. He used to fly into the most terrible rages. He was excluded for attacking a teacher."

"What was the argument about?" Chris asked.

Mr Harris' answer punched right into his stomach.

"The customer wasn't happy about McLeish's pet mouse."

"Mouse?"

"Yes, it seems he had a pet mouse. He took it everywhere with him."

"Where is he now?" Chris asked, recovering a little. "McLeish, I mean, not the mouse."

"Oh, he's six feet under," said Mr Harris. "He died in prison. He had a fight with another inmate. Good riddance, I say. The day he was excluded from school he said he'd come back to get me. He never did, but I still can't get that moment out of my mind. The time he said that to me, it was the only moment in my whole life I've been truly terrified. He said he'd come back from the grave to get me if he had to."

Chris had one final question, though he already knew the answer.

"This McLeish," he said. "What job did he do?"

Mr Harris gave the photo a last look.

"He was a computer technician."

7

It was Parents' Evening.

"Can't I come with you?" Chris asked.

Mum looked at him as though he'd just come

into the room wearing a red nose and riding a unicycle.

"You're usually dead keen to get us out of the house," she said, "so you can have the place to yourself. Since when did you want to come to Parents' Evening with us?'"

Since you bought me a psycho computer, Chris thought. But he didn't say so.

Instead he repeated the question: "So can I come?"

"Don't be daft," said Dad. "The school made a big point in the letter about parents not bringing their kids along. No, you stay in and watch a bit of telly. Or play on that computer."

Chris's skin prickled at the thought but he accepted defeat quietly. All I have to do, he told himself, is stay down here and watch TV. If I don't go in my room what can the computer possibly do? So there he sat. But he didn't watch TV. He couldn't make sense of the pictures on the screen. All the time he was listening for the tell-tale sounds of the computer. In the end he turned off the TV and sat waiting to see what the computer was going to do. Ten minutes later he started to discover exactly what it had in mind. The first sign that anything was wrong was when something scuttered across the floor and the lights dimmed.

"Mum?" said Chris. "Dad?"

There was no reply. He knew it wasn't them but he carried on asking anyway. "Is there anybody in?"

As if in reply the TV fizzed to life. Chris stared at the screen. Then he noticed that it was getting warmer. He went to check the central heating. It was on maximum.

"This is your doing, isn't it, McLeish?"

Chris heard something in the kitchen. He walked in and stopped dead in his tracks. The whole room was alive with electrical activity. The microwave was glowing. The oven was on. The kettle was boiling. The strip light stuttered. Just as Chris was taking it all in, a loud pop made him jump. It was the toaster.

"OK," said Chris. "Very clever. What's your next party trick?"

The moment the words were out of his mouth he felt sick. What am I trying to do, Chris thought, challenge him to do his worst?

"Stupid!"

Then he heard music playing in the living room. It was an old Sinatra track:

"...saying something stupid like I love you..."

"Oh that does it," said Chris. "I'm going to put a stop to this for good and all."

The track changed on the CD player. The new tune was:

"A little mouse with clogs on, going clip, clippety clop on the stairs."

Then, as Chris got to the top of the stairs, it changed again, to:

"Wild thing."

"Oh, very funny," said Chris.

He saw the words on the computer screen:

You think so?

They were accompanied by a piece of clip-art: the skull and crossbones.

Chris wanted to hit back, to show the computer he

wasn't going to be intimidated. Even though it hadn't worked the last time he did it, he yanked the plugs from the wall. This time the PC didn't shut down, not even for an instant. Then Chris knew what he had to do.

Go on then, the computer screen read; **show me what you've got**.

Oh, I will, Chris thought. I certainly will.

He flew to the electricity cupboard and pulled the fuses. The house lights died.

"Gotcha!"

With a victory cry, Chris raced upstairs.

"Gotcha! Gotcha! Gotcha!"

But, when he walked into his room, the words died in his throat.

The computer screen was lit and there was a message:

Don't gotcha.

8

Chris stared in disbelief.

Don't gotcha; that's what it said.

"That's it," Chris said. "I've had enough."

He ran to the phone to call Mum and Dad. The line was dead. Dead for a few seconds, that is. Then an electronic voice crackled down the line:

Don't gotcha.

Suddenly Chris wasn't frightened. He was angry. He was defiant.

"Oh, don't I?"

Now he had a battle plan. First, arm yourself. Second, call for help. He walked into the kitchen.

The lights came on around him but he ignored them. Opening the kitchen drawer, he pulled out the hammer Mum and Dad used for household jobs. Then, switching on his mobile, he started keying in the numbers to Mum's.

"Gotcha," he said loudly. "Gotcha, don't I McLeish?"

The reply came in a chorus of electronic noises. The house came alive with a cannonade of sound. The TV and CD player blared, the toaster popped, the kettle boiled. Chris could hear the shower, the answer machine, the alarm clock.

"Is that all you've got?" Chris yelled over the whoop of the burglar alarm.

He put the phone to his ear. That's when a blinding pain shot through his arm. He dropped the phone. He could hear Mum's voice:

"Hello? Chris? Hello?"

He reached for the phone. That's when he saw big, heavy drops of blood forming at the ends of his fingertips. A pair of scissors was embedded in his upper arm and a thin stream of blood oozed from the wound.

"How?" he wondered out loud as he eased the blades from his flesh and held a bandage to the gash.

That did it. It was kill or be killed. His arm still aching, Chris took the stairs two at a time and made for the computer. He raised the hammer, but the computer wasn't finished. The screen flashed and a bulb exploded overhead, showering him with glass. Next moment the same happened to his bedside lamp. Chris wasn't to be put off by a few party tricks.

He swung the hammer again. This time the computer screen shattered. The machine fought back. Chris felt an electronic shock run the length of his body. The shudder cascaded down his spine. But he wasn't going to stop. He swung the hammer again and again.

When his worried parents pulled up in front of the house Chris was already dumping the mangled PC in the skip across the road.

"What the hell are you doing?" Dad cried, staring the wreckage of the computer. "Do you know what I paid for that thing? Have you gone mad?"

"No Dad," Chris said. "I've just come to my senses."

9

Mum and Dad never did believe him about the PC. He was grounded for a month and there was some talk of psychologists but, in the end, the whole incident was quietly forgotten. There was no new computer and Chris didn't mind one bit. He didn't care if he didn't have a PC ever. Six weeks later he was looking forward to the new football season. He was even looking forward to the new school year.

It started on a sunny September morning. Chris almost bounced through the school gates. But there, to his surprise, he was met by a crowd of students.

"What's going on?" he asked Sean.

"Haven't you heard? It's old Harris. He crashed his car on the way to school this morning. He's dead."

"Mr Harris," Chris said, darkness flooding through him. "He's dead? Are you sure?"

"Positive."

"Jeez."

Chris stared at the ground.

"Jeez."

"You know what's really weird," Sean said. "He had his laptop on in the passenger seat."

"How do you know?"

"One of the girls in Year Nine found him," Sean said. "You know what's really weird?"

Chris remembered what Mr Harris had told him weeks before.

He came back to get you, didn't he?

Chris could hardly force the next word through the lump in his throat. The question echoed through his mind. You know what's really weird?

"What?"

"There was one word on the computer screen. You know what it was?"

Chris shuddered. It was as if a mouse's tiny feet were running over his skin. He knew what the message would be, and he was right.

"Gotcha."